Andrew Halliday

Adventures of Mr. Wilderspin on His Journey Through Life

Andrew Halliday

Adventures of Mr. Wilderspin on His Journey Through Life

ISBN/EAN: 9783337011154

Printed in Europe, USA, Canada, Australia, Japan

Cover: Foto ©Andreas Hilbeck / pixelio.de

More available books at **www.hansebooks.com**

ADVENTURES

OF

M^R. WILDERSPIN

ON HIS

JOURNEY THROUGH LIFE.

BY

ANDREW HALLIDAY.

NUMEROUS ILLUSTRATIONS.

FIFTH EDITION.

LONDON:
WARD, LOCK AND TYLER,
WARWICK HOUSE, PATERNOSTER ROW.

CONTENTS.

ADVENTURE THE FIRST.

ADVENTURE THE SECOND.

ADVENTURE THE THIRD.

ADVENTURE THE FOURTH.

ADVENTURE THE FIFTH.

ADVENTURE THE SIXTH.

ADVENTURE THE SEVENTH.

ADVENTURE THE EIGHTH.

ADVENTURE THE NINTH.

ADVENTURE THE TENTH.

ADVENTURE THE THIRTEENTH.

ADVENTURE THE FOURTEENTH.

ADVENTURE THE FIFTEENTH.

ADVENTURE THE SIXTEENTH.

ADVENTURE THE SEVENTEENTH.

ADVENTURE THE EIGHTEENTH.

ADVENTURE THE NINETEENTH.

ADVENTURE THE TWENTIETH.

ADVENTURE THE TWENTY-THIRD AND LAST.

THE

ADVENTURES OF MR. WILDERSPIN,

On His Journey through Life.

ADVENTURE THE FIRST.

Mr. Wilderspin, a Railway Clerk with ideas above his station-reads of "something to his advantage."—Hears of the "something," which proves to be a legacy of £8000 left by a relation in Australia—of course a distant relation.—The wheels of fortune having turned up a prize, Mr. Wilderspin becomes temporarily cranky.—Takes counsel of a Q. C. (queer customer), a friend of sporting tastes, who advises him to institute several suits (new), and to invest in A good stock.—Mr. Wilderspin having found himself heir to property, tries the properties of Mr. Grossmith's "Nardia" in finding hairs to his chin—Comes out a heavy swell, but finding his acquaintance incline to make light of his appearance tries—A swell of the first water, but being voted by the boys in the street a pump, resolves no longer to afford a handle to the remarks of the impertinent, and—Rigs himself out in the New (market) Cut.—Considers himself at last "the cheese," and is mightily pleased with his appearance.—In company with his sporting friend Tipton, he starts to see life at the Cattle Show.

It has been frequently observed, that the life of any man, no matter how humble or insignificant in station he may be, cannot fail, if faithfully recorded, to prove both interesting and instructive. Regarding this as an incontrovertible axiom, the present writer enters upon

B

the task of recording the Adventures of Mr. Wilderspin,
in the confident hope, that, though the subject of his
biographical efforts may not have made himself a great
name by the exercise of his genius in any of those walks
of life in which men win distinction and honour, he may
nevertheless attract the attention, and secure the favour
of the public, in respect of those personal and mental
qualities, which have so eminently distinguished him,
and so greatly endeared him to all who have had the
pleasure of his society.   Upon Mr. Wilderspin's early
career it will not be necessary to dwell, further than to
state, that, like many other distinguished persons whose
lives have been written, he was "born of poor but respectable parents," that he was a youth of restless ambition, who outgrew the clothes of his infancy and boy-
hood very fast, and who, shortly after a borough election, at which his father voted for the Liberal candidate,
found himself appointed to a railway clerkship in London, at an exceedingly moderate salary.   Mr. Wilderspin, though constitutionally of a modest and retiring
nature, was at an early period impressed with the conviction that he was possessed of genius ; and from the
time that he cast off the jacket of youth to assume the
"tails" of maturity, he longed for an opportunity of
distinguishing himself.   A very few days' experience
in the office of the railway company convinced him
that his genius did not lie in the direction of figures,
or neat book-keeping : his senior in the department was
convinced of this fact even before it began to dawn

upon Mr. Wilderspin himself. If there was anything for which Mr. Wilderspin seemed in the eyes of his senior to have a genius, it was for making blots on the ledger, and committing errors in his addition sums. Neither the mantle of Carstairs nor that of Cocker had fallen upon Mr. Wilderspin. What might have been the result to Mr. Wilderspin of these blots and inaccurate sums total, had he remained in the office for any length of time, is a point we may guess at, if we cannot positively settle and determine ; but it was the good fortune of Mr. Wilderspin to be suddenly emancipated from the thraldom of the railway office. One forenoon when he had made an awful blot on the ledger, and added up the shillings of a coal account with the pounds of the same, he rushed away in great perplexity of mind to clear his faculties with a little refreshment. Mr. Wilderspin was accustomed to clear his faculties with a little refreshment every day at twelve, noon ; and while treating his physical man to such recruitment as is afforded by saveloys, it was his constant practice to stay his mental cravings with the intellectual pabulum provided in the Supplement to the *Times* newspaper. On this occasion, after undergoing the usual course of catechetical and admonitory advice with respect to his oats, his teas, his carpets, his perambulator, &c., few of which articles he used or *required*, any more than he did a vent-peg, Mr. Wilderspin's eye fell upon something near the top of the third column of the front page, which had the effect of sending a bit of saveloy down

MR. WILDERSPIN, A RAILWAY CLERK WITH IDEAS ABOVE HIS STATION, READS OF " SOMETHING TO HIS ADVANTAGE."

HEARS OF THE SAID "SOMETHING," WHICH PROVES TO BE A LEGACY OF £8000 LEFT BY A RELATION IN AUSTRALIA—OF COURSE A DISTANT RELATION.

THE WHEEL OF FORTUNE HAVING TURNED UP A PRIZE, MR. WILDERSPIN BE-
COMES TEMPORARILY CRANKY.

TAKES COUNSEL OF A Q.C., (QUEER CUSTOMER), A FRIEND OF SPORTING TASTES,
WHO ADVISES HIM TO INSTITUTE SEVERAL SUITS, (NEW,) AND TO INVEST IN

his throat the wrong way, and very nearly causing him
to choke. Having with the aid of a half a pint of
porter, partially recovered his breath and his faculties,
Mr. Wilderspin again cast his eye upon the top of the
third column. There was no mistake about it : there,
in large capitals fully displayed, was his own name—
WILDERSPIN ! The advertisement proceeded to say,
that if Horatio Wilderspin, eldest son of Ebenezer Wilderspin, would apply at the office of Mr. Scraggs, solicitor, of No. 9, Cross Square, he would hear of something to his advantage. Mr. Wilderspin read this over
at least a dozen times—without winking, or apparently
drawing a breath. Two or three persons had said
" After you with the paper, Sir ;" but he took no notice
of them, and stood like one transfixed, until a sudden
thought seemed to strike him, when he dashed down
the paper, flourished his umbrella over his head, and
uttering a wild hurrah ! rushed from the tavern. In
his excitement Mr. Wilderspin had forgotten to pay
for his refreshment—a circumstance to which the
strangeness of his conduct did not, however, render
the landlord oblivious. That person immediately jumped
over the bar, and started in pursuit of the defaulter,
which gave the customers who remained occasion to
discover that it was time to be back at business. So
that the upshot of the pursuit of Mr. Wilderspin was a
practical illustration of the proverb that "a bird in the
hand is worth two in the bush ;" for while beating the
the bush for Mr Wilderspin's fivepence, the worthy

licensed victualler found, to his mortification and loss, that a half a dozen birds—whose aggregate value was considerable—had made their escape.

This first incident in Mr. Wilderspin's life gave an augury of that adventurous career which distinguished the course of his after-existence. Nelson first gave evidence of his daring spirit by robbing an orchard; Napoleon by conducting a snow-battle at Brienne ; Mr. Wilderspin by conducting himself in a manner that enabled half a dozen city clerks to get their luncheon for nothing.

Mr. Wilderspin, quite regardless of office hours, proceeded at once to the address of Mr. Scraggs in Cross Square. The door of Mr. Scraggs's office occupied a dark corner of the square, and was not unsuggestive of the web of a spider. Indeed, a good many human flies, who had incautiously flown into it, found that this was no metaphor. Mr. Wilderspin, on being introduced to Mr. Scraggs's den, discovered that gentleman perched upon a very high stool, in an attitude decidedly entomological. He was evidently accustomed to assume that position, in order that he might more conveniently dart down the line when a tremulous motion of his web indicated that a fly was fast in his meshes. Mr. Scraggs was not disposed to admit too readily that the Wilderspin before him was the Wilderspin he was instructed to search for ; and though he was forced to admit it at length, he took good care that the progress of proving the same should be slow, and should at the same time

A GOOD STOCK.

MR. WILDERSPIN HAVING FOUND HIMSELF HEIR TO PROPERTY, TRIES THE PRO-
PERTIES OF MR. GROSSMITH'S "NARDIA," IN FINDING HAIRS TO HIS CHIN.

COMES OUT A HEAVY SWELL, BUT FINDING
HIS ACQUAINTANCE INCLINED TO MAKE
LIGHT OF HIS APPEARANCE, TRIES

A SWELL OF THE FIRST WATER, BUT
BEING VOTED BY THE BOYS IN
THE STREET A PUMP, RESOLVES
NO LONGER TO AFFORD A HANDLE
TO THE REMARKS OF THE IMPER-
TINENT, AND

RIGS HIMSELF OUT IN THE NEW-
(MARKET) CUT.

involve the writing of many letters and the holding of many interviews with his client.

It would not be a profitable employment of space to detail the tedious process of proof, by baptismal register and otherwise, by which is was established that our hero, Mr. Horatio Wilderspin, was the true heir to a sum of £8,000, left to him by the will of his deceased uncle, Ebenezer Wilderspin, of Ballarat, New South Wales : suffice it to say that it was established, and that Mr. Horatio Wilderspin came into possession of that sum minus about £500, retained by Mr. Scraggs in satisfaction of costs. Mr. Wilderspin in the mean time, had abdicated his high stool in the railway office, and his employers, in parting with him, were pleased to say, that though he had left many blots upon the ledger, there was no blot whatever upon his character ; and that though it might be desirable that many of his entries should be erased from the books generally, there was nothing in his conduct and behaviour, while in their service, that they could wish erased from their memories.

Mr. Wilderspin, being now in possession of nearly £8,000 in hard cash, resolved to see and enjoy life, confidently hoping that, being fully emancipated from all ties of duty to any one but himself, he would soon discover a field for the display of those superior powers which he secretly believed himself to possess. Walking home to his two-pair back in Bloomsbury, with all this money in his pocket, he was, however, not a little puz-

zled to know how to begin. It occurred to him once
or twice, that he would only be following the dictates
of human nature if he were to treat himself to a bottle
of champagne. Then he thought of buying a silver-
mounted meerchaum. Next it came into his head that
a white hat, with crape round it, would be something
exactly consonant with his sudden state of wealth.
Turning a certain street corner, it occurred to him that, as
a man of principle, it would, perhaps, be most meritori-
ous if he began by paying his boot-maker, to whom he
owed 11s. 6d., for some neatly executed repairs. Mr.
Wilderspin revolved these projects in his mind, one
after the other, without being able to decide upon any
of them ; but, meeting with his friend Tipton, a gentleman of sporting tastes, he was soon put in the right
course. Tipton was a slap-dash sort of fellow, who
had made up his mind on every subject, not in consequence of having well and thoroughly weighed and
studied every subject, but because he had very little
mind to make up. And yet, what there was of Mr.
Tipton's mind was not of a bad quality, and it was
made up in a very neat parcel. "Take my advice,"
said Tipton ; "begin by laying in a good stock of togs :
if it ever were true that it is the tailor that makes the
man, it is true in these days. All classes, my dear boy,
respect the tailor. Who is it that finds favour with the
girls? The swell. Who is it that gets the situation which
a hundred fellows are after ? The man with the dashing, confident air, which he derives from his good suit

of clothes, and his knowledge that his watch and chain will stand the test of aqua fortis. Who is it that gets tick? Not the out-at-elbows chap, with a dingy shirt-front, and his boots down at heel. No, sir; the man of good exterior, who is wide awake enough, even if it taxes him a little, to put on a clean shirt on Saturdays! Who are the men who marry women with money?—who captivate warm widows?—who run away with heiresses?—who attract the eyes of Countesses in the park? In fact, who are the men who get on in the world? Is it your slouching, seedy fellows, with greasy coat-collars and shocking bad hats? No! It is the men who appear every day as if they had just come out of a band-box—the men who wear good clothes fashionably cut, and sport well-curled whiskers."

Mr. Wilderspin was deeply impressed with this exhortation, the force of which he fully perceived; but though his wealth could undoubtedly command the most fashionable attire, he was not aware that he had it in his power to compel nature to clothe his cheeks with well-curled whiskers. Mr. Tipton, however, made his mind easy on that score, by assuring him that there were various specifics, which he knew of, which would speedily produce the desired result; and this assurance Mr. Wilderspin's confiding nature trustfully accepted, notwithstanding that it did not escape his observation that Mr. Tipton's own cheeks could not boast a single hair. Mr. Wilderspin took his friend Tipton's advice, and immediately laid in a good stock of the requisites of a

CONSIDERS HIMSELF AT LAST "THE CHEESE," AND IS MIGHTILY PLEASED WITH
HIS APPEARANCE.

IN COMPANY WITH HIS SPORTING FRIEND TIPTON, HE STARTS TO SEE LIFE AT
THE CATTLE SHOW.

gentleman's toilet.   He had long been ambitious of
cutting a swell, and now he was enabled to gratify his aspirations to the fullest extent.   After an evening's shop-
ping, under the friendly guidance of Tipton, his apartment presented an appearance similar to that of an Ameri-
can store.   In confusion, anything but picturesque, there
was collected together Paris hats, and shaving-paste,
patent-leather boots and briar-root pipes, revolvers and
white kid gloves, razors and soda-water, pomatum and
patent coffee-pots, boot-jacks, cigars, canes, bottles of
scent, volumes of hints on etiquette, and a hundred
other articles besides,—not omitting a bottle of fluid,
warranted to produce a handsome pair of whiskers after
a few applications, the properties of which Mr. Wilderspin lost no time in putting to the test—but with no
other immediate result than that of discolouring his
cheeks and making them smart very much.

Having resolved that the first duty of his position
was to become a swell, Mr. Wilderspin had his measure
taken for various styles of apparel.   He had hitherto
been accustomed to so little variety of costume, that he
was unable to determine in what fashion of clothing he
would appear to the greatest advantage.   Being a man
of small stature, he had naturally been prone to admire
the style of costume adopted by big men.   It had often
struck him, that if he could endue himself in a full-
bodied coat with broad lappels, double seams, and wide
sleeves, and at the same time mount a hat with some
breadth of brim, he would not feel so small in the street

beside men of five-feet-ten or so. He tried this style first; but Mr. Tipton and others having remarked that the suit fitted him all over and touched him nowhere, and the boys in the street having on several occasions commanded him in a peremptory manner to "Come out of that hat!" he began to suspect, that whatever sort of swell might be his *role*, it was not the heavy swell. The new semi-clerical Oxford coat next took his fancy. It was a garment that had suddenly become very popular, in connexion with High Church principles, and a slim umbrella. Mr. Wilderspin was rather pleased with himself in this costume; and strange to say, on the first Sunday after putting it on, he found himself, by some mysterious influence, attracted to a place of worship where they chaunted the service, and decorated the altar with candles and flowers. Mr. Wilderspin might have rested quite satisfied with this style of costume, had he not shortly had occasoin to suspect that Tipton was what is popularly called "chaffing," him, when, in asking him to shake hands, he made use of the expression, "Give me your handle, old Pump!" Some random remarks of those inexorable censors, the boys, and the sight of his shadow on the wall one night, brought the conviction to Mr. Wilderspin's mind, that Mr. Tipton's remark about a pump had an application to himself not altogether flattering. In consequence of this discovery, he appeared in the Oxford toga no more and his biographer has reason to believe that it was nearly about the same time that he discontinued his visits to the fashionable church already mentioned ; which leads the said biographer to inquire, if the coat which is said to make the man secularly, and in a physical point of view, does not sometimes make the man spiritual ?

Mr. Wilderspin came to the conclusion at last, that the style which was most adapted both to his figure and his feelings, was that which partakes not so much of the heavy swell, or the mild drawing-room swell, as of the gent, or the man about town. He selected a close-fitting coat, with pockets and large buttons, a pair of continuations fitting closely to his legs, a hat with a narrow brim, and, with a pink neck-tie, fastened by a horse-shoe pin, he was complete, and entirely to his own satisfaction. That he was right in his choice this time he was warranted in believing, by the fact that he now entirely escaped criticism.

Mr. Wilderspin had by this time provided himself with lodgings more becoming his means and position, and was happy in finding Mr, Tipton a close attendant upon all his excursions in pursuit of pleasure. Mr. Wilderspin's difficulty was not that of my Lord Tom Noddy ; he had not exhausted all the fields of Elysium, and become a wearied searcher after new sensations. His difficulty was, that the fields of pleasure which now lay before him were so many, and all of them so new to him, that he could not make up his mind which to explore first. Being in this dilemma on a nice sloppy, foggy, December morning, when most of the fields might be expected to be damp, Mr. Wilderspin received a visit from the ever-faithful Tipton, who, after being refreshed with something short, as a preventative against the effects of the rain, proposed a visit to the Cattle Show. "Was puzzling my brains, as I came along this morning," said Tipton, "what we should be up to, and couldn't think of anything that one could enjoy in such confounded weather, until I began to observe that there were a great many red-cheeked, beefy looking men about the streets, chaps with great hobnailed boots and furry hats; you know the sort. What could it be, thought I, that has brought us all this mud and slush and all those beefy-looking country chaps? Why, the Cattle Show of course! Was there ever a Cattle Show without rain and mud, and fat men? So come along, old boy! let us be off to Baker Street!"

Mr. Wilderspin was not a judge of prize oxen or pigs, save in their beef and pork stage; but being assured that the Show was a capital place to see human, as well as brute life, he lighted his medium Emperor, and chartering a cab—of course, a Hansom—drove off with his friend Tipton to Baker Street.

ADVENTURE THE SECOND.

Mr. Wilderspin, having admired the proportions of Mr. Heath's
Hereford Ox, turns to admire the *proportions* of other animals
in the Show.—Taking a fancy to Mr. J. V. Williams's pen of
pigs, he is accosted by "two gentlemen from the country," who
know the breeder, and point out the "points" of the prize
animal.—The "two gentlemen from the country" take a great
fancy to Mr. Wilderspin.—Mr. Wilderspin and the "two gentlemen from the country" adjourn to a neighbouring tavern,
and drink to their better acquaintance.—Mr. Wilderspin, after
a few glasses of *rather peculiar* ale, finds himself playing skittles with the "two gentlemen from the country," and winning.
—The "two gentlemen from the country" *suddenly improve* in
their play, and Mr. Wilderspin loses.—Comes to his last stake,
and feels himself very small.—When he is fairly cleaned out,
Mr. Wilderspin at last gets a "*floorer*."

THE neighbourhood of Baker Street at Cattle Show
time presents a scene of as complete discomfort as can
well be imagined.   It always rains at Cattle Show time:
there is always mud at Cattle Show time—and Baker
Street being the centre of attraction at that period, it
follows that the crowd there is a damp crowd, and consequently an uncomfortable crowd.   Many a poor
threadpaper cockney catches cold by sitting next to a
damp farmer in an Atlas omnibus at Cattle Show time.
That rubicund gentleman in the top-boots and velveteen
jacket has damp enough about him to supply influenza
to a dozen cockneys: on himself it takes no effect.

What does take effect upon that man? Look at the
steaks he eats : no, not eats—puts away! Does he
wink, or turn a hair? Not he. Look at the beer he
drinks ; but there!—you haven't time to look at it: it
is gone before you can say "Jack Robinson," or, shall
I say, "Meux." Mr. Wilderspin was much impressed
with the prevailing British farmer element, and, like all
men of small frame and feeble physical power, he could
not resist something like envy of their solid proportions
and complete imperviousness to all outward influences.
On regarding the British farmer by the side of his ox,
his pig, his sheep, and every four-footed thing in the
Show that was his, it dimly occurred to Mr. Wilderspin
that the excellent condition of the British farmer might
be referable to the absence of that intellectual wear and
tear which left him, equally with the four-footed beast,
entirely free to devote himself to the task of getting
fat. If I have not mentioned it before, I had better
mention it now, that Mr. Wilderspin's mind was of a
philosophical cast. He was in the habit of (inwardly)
making many sagacious remarks upon men and things,
and if his friends did not give him credit for that
amount of intellectual grasp which he really possessed,
it was because he had not yet acquired the habit of
expressing himself. On this occasion, however, he was
moved to attempt a little moralizing, for the benefit of
his friend Tipton. "You will observe, Tipton," said
Mr. Wilderspin—leaning over the shoulder of the prize
Hereford ox—"you will observe a wonderful, ah--a

wonderful resemblance I may say, not absolutely in feature, but in the general style and appearance—ah—between that ox and his master." This thought had evidently taken a very profound shape in Mr. Wilderspin's brain, and he was much relieved when he had given it oral birth.

"Well, if you mean that they are both fat," said Tipton, flippantly, not at all in a philosophic manner, "there *is* a resemblance." "But did it never strike you, Tipton," continued Mr. Wilderspin, "that—that the nature of a man's occupation, say the tending of oxen, may have a tendency to assimilate,"—Mr. Wilderspin was getting on capitally—"to assimilate his aspect—yes, his aspect—with—in fact—his occupation, or the object of his occupation?"

"What do you mean?" inquired Tipton.

"Ah!" said Mr. Wilderspin, "I see I have not explained myself quite clearly; I will just put the case again."

And Mr. Wilderspin placed his finger on his nose in an excogitative attitude.

"Now look here, Wilderspin!" said Tipton, before his friend could get any further; "none of this, I can't bear sermonizing, and I never thought you would take to that; don't talk about assimilating, and that sort of thing. I am no philosopher, old boy; let's look at the girls."

"They appear," said Mr. Wilderspin, "to form no inconsiderable part of the Show;" rather disgusted

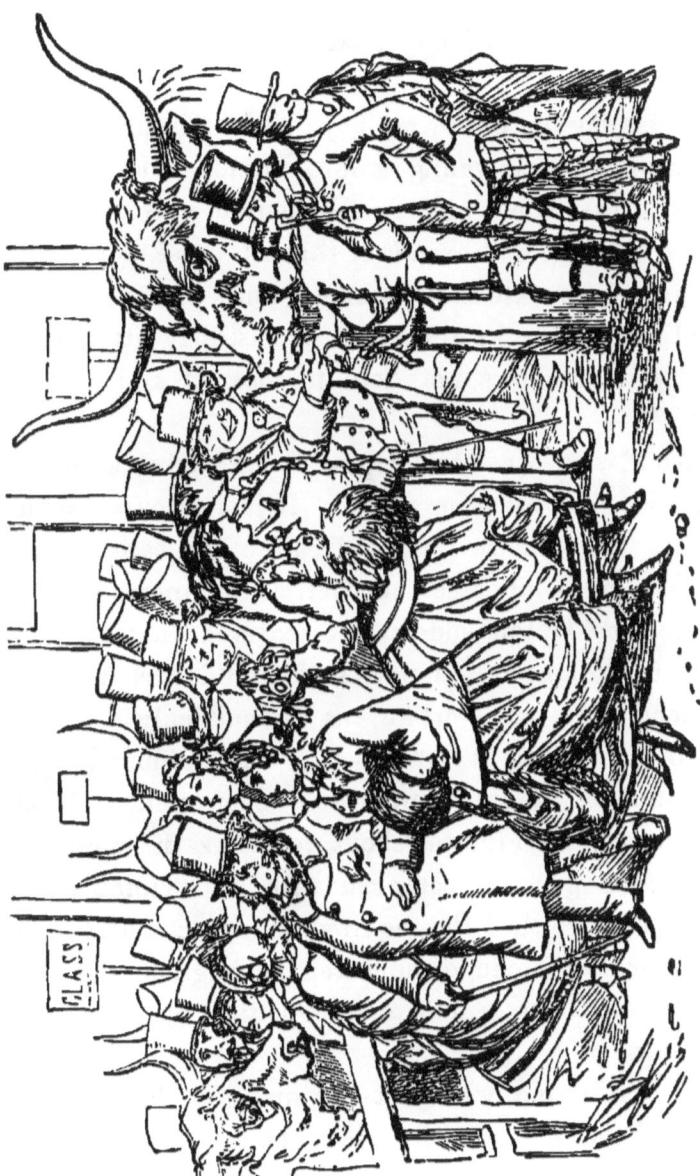

MR. WILDERSPIN HAVING ADMIRED THE PROPORTIONS OF MR. HEATH'S HEREFORD OX, TURNS TO ADMIRE THE PROPORTIONS OF OTHER ANIMALS IN THE SHOW.

with Tipton's want of appreciation of his first effort to be philosophical.

"They *are* the Show, my boy;" said Tipton. "Do you think all these young fellows would come here in patent-leather boots and straw-coloured gloves merely to look at sheep and oxen? or that all those delightful creatures in cockle-shell bonnets and lace petticoats would risk their silks and satins in this dirty litter, were these young fellows not here to look at and admire them?"

"Ah!" said Mr. Wilderspin, "your remark opens up a wide field for observation. It just occurs to me that the same remark may apply in other cases. For example: at fashionable churches, at the opera, at—"

Here Mr. Tipton suddenly discovered that he had come out without any money, and would Mr. Wilderspin lend him half-a-crown, as he suddenly felt the need of something to drink. Mr. Wilderspin, though rather hurt at the interruption to a deep philosophical observation which he was about to make in reference to things in general, complied with Mr. Tipton's request, and furnished the required amount; whereupon the latter gentleman disappeared with great alacrity, leaving Mr. Wilderspin in contemplation of a pen of prize pigs.

Mr. Wilderspin was just beginning to have some profound thoughts about porcine habits, manners, and customs, when he became aware of the close proximity of two gentlemen of provincial aspect, whose close attention to his philosophical conversation with Tipton would have flattered him, had he only been aware of it.

" You have evidently an eye for a pig, sir ;" said the taller of the two, addressing Mr. Wilderspin.

For a moment or two, Mr. Wilderspin was not quite sure if it would be a creditable thing to admit that he had an eye for a pig ; but the other gentleman remarking that it was a useful animal, he was to a certain extent relieved of his difficulty, and returned that it *was* a useful animal, undoubtedly.

" Not very handsome, perhaps, but yet the animal had its points of beauty."

Mr. Wilderspin said, " No doubt."

" For example, that animal, which was the prize pig, had its points of beauty."

Mr. Wilderspin said, " Oh, decidedly !"

" It could not see out of its eyes, that was one thing."

" Indeed !" said Mr. Wilderspin.

" No ;" proceeded the tall man, " and another thing, it could not stand on its legs."

Mr. Wilderspin said, " Really."

" And what's more," said the shorter man, an individual with a wide awake and a serpentine walking-stick, " he could not get up now if it could save himself from being made bacon of."

" Bacon !" said Mr. Wilderspin, an idea striking him ; " bacon—that is the end of his mission upon earth ; is it not ?"

The tall man was pleased to say, in a facetious manner, that it was bacon ; whereupon his friend struck in
and said, " And no gammon !"

Mr. Wilderspin replied, " As you correctly observed,
and no gammon ;" when the two gentlemen, of provincial aspect, immediately went into fits of laughter,
swearing, when they had fully recovered, that Mr.
Wilderspin was both a philosopher and a wag. It was
not, of course, for Mr. Wilderspin to reply to such an
insinuation, but by his approving smiles he appeared
to own the soft impeachment.

" As I observed before, sir," said the tall man, " you
have evidently an eye for a pig."

Mr. Wilderspin having now begun to see that it was
in a philosophical and artistic sense that this was meant,
did not mind owning that he had an eye for a pig."

" Now, sir," continued the tall man, " if you were
to cut into that pig, what would you see ?"

It passed vaguely through Mr. Wilderspin's mind
that he might see blood ; but he did not like to be rash,
lest that should be the wrong answer.

The tall gentleman relieved him from his dilemma by
answering the question himself.

" Why, nothing but fat ! That pig, sir, has only one
streak of fat in his whole body, and that combined with
his inability to see, stand, or even grunt, was what made
a prize pig of him."

The shorter gentleman here asked, "if it wasn't
shameful ?"

TAKING A FANCY TO MR. J. V. WILLIAMS'S PEN OF PIGS, HE IS ACCOSTED BY "TWO GENTLEMEN FROM THE COUNTRY," WHO KNOW THE BREEDER. THEY TAKE A GREAT FANCY TO MR. WILDERSPIN.

THEY ADJOURN TO A TAVERN, AND DRINK TO THEIR BETTER ACQUAINTANCE.

Mr. Wilderspin, who now began to see the direction of these remarks, answered, upon some little reflection, that it was ; he thought for purposes of bacon the prize pig could be of little avail, that therefore the food which had been bestowed upon him, had been wasted ; and this led him to dilate upon the iniquity of overfeeding animals merely to produce a degree of fatness, which was of no practical benefit to mankind, while there were many human beings who would be glad of the overflowing of that pig's trough. At the conclusion of these remarks, the two gentlemen of provincial aspect, said, simultaneously, that it was evident to them that Mr. Wilderspin was a man of sense and observation.

Mr. Wilderspin's new acquaintances being themselves obviously exhibitors, were well acquainted with all the interesting features of the Show, and were good enough to direct Mr. Wilderspin's attention to whatever was worth seeing. After reviewing the oxen, the pigs, and the sheep, he went up stairs, accompanied by his friends, and witnessed a variety of ruthless-looking machines for performing a multiplicity of agricultural functions, very few of which, he was assured, they did perform anything like decently. He had also the pleasure of inspecting various specimens of wheat, barley, oats, peas, beans, &c., some of which articles of produce were not altogether familiar to him in the shape they then presented. The end of this perambulation was, that Mr. Wilderspin and the two exhibitors became very friendly, and agreed to adjourn to a neighbouring tavern to drink to better acquaintance.

"What would Mr. Wilderspin take?"

Mr. Wilderspin was one of those delicate-minded men who never liked to wound the sensibilities of his friends by appearing to be in any way their superior. Sherry would have been the drink in consonance with his means and position, but, suspecting that his friends were more modest in their tastes, he asked what they said to ale? Ale was just the thing; and one of the gentlemen condescended to fetch a quart from the bar, being unwilling, as he said, to trouble the waiter, whose exertions were evidently overtaxed by the rush of Cattle Show customers. When the ale was brought in, a pleasant struggle ensued between Mr. Wilderspin and the tall gentleman as to which should pay for the refreshment. Mr. Wilderspin pulled out a purse tolerably well lined with sovereigns, and, almost at the same moment, the tall gentleman produced a pocket-book bursting with notes. The victory, that is, to say the privilege of paying—eventually fell to Mr. Wilderspin, much, as it appeared, to the tall gentleman's disappointment.

The tall gentleman was of opinion that it was a good glass of ale. The gentleman with the serpentine stick, held his glass up to the light, and eyeing it cunningly, pronounced the ale "sound."

Mr. Wilderspin acquiesced in the judgment, but added, after emptying his glass—"Heady, rather."

MR. WILDERSPIN AFTER A FEW GLASSES OF RATHER PECULIAR ALE, FINDS HIMSELF PLAYING SKITTLES WITH THE "TWO GENTLEMEN FROM THE COUNTRY," AND WINNING.

THE "TWO GENTLEMEN FROM THE COUNTRY," SUDDENLY IMPROVE IN THEIR
PLAY, AND MR. WILDERSPIN LOSES.

COMES TO HIS LAST STAKE, AND FEELS
HIMSELF VERY SMALL.

His friends thought not ; but dear, dear, it was raining again, absolutely pouring. How were they to pass the afternoon ? The tall gentleman yawned and said, he had no idea; unless they went back to the Show. His friend objected to that—he was tired of it. Mr. Wilderspin suggested waiting until the rain left off, when he would have great pleasure in taking his country friends to see some of the sights, say the British Museum. His friends said that *would* be a treat indeed ; but unfortunately the rain did not give the slightest symptom of leaving off.

Suddenly a brilliant idea struck the gentleman with the serpentine walking-stick. Suppose they were to play a game of skittles; he ebserved that a "good dry ground" was attached to the house.

The tall gentleman was delighted with the notion ; what did Mr. Wilderspin say.

Well, that gentleman was fond of athletic sports, and he did not mind confessing that skittles had a charm for him, and moreover, that he could play a little.

Well, as far as that went, the tall gentleman could own to a liking for the game, but, he was sorry to say, he was no great dabster at it. His friend was afraid that he was not much of a hand either ; but still, he had no doubt they could all play well enough to amuse themselves. Now, if the truth must be told, Mr. Wilderspin had had some practice at skittles, and rather prided himself upon his skill at the game. He, consequently, did not require much pressing to adjourn to the ground. His first throw showed his friends that he was not unused to the practice of the game. The ball was exceedingly well intended, and not so successful as it deserved.

"I can see with half an eye, sir," said the tall gentleman, "that it is not the first time you have thrown a ball."

"No, nor yet the second;" said the other gentleman.

Mr. Wilderspin was pleased and encouraged by these flattering remarks.

In the first game, Mr. Wilderspin won an easy victory over both his friends.

The tall gentleman then said, addressing Mr. W., "You'll excuse us, sir, but my friend and I are accustomed to stake a trifle when we play together, just to give interest to the thing, you know ; but that needn't interfere with you, sir."

The other gentleman said, "No ; it needn't interfere with Mr. Wilderspin." The game was resumed, and Mr. Wilderspin still continued to exhibit superior skill. He was aware that if he hit the foremost of the nine pins on the right shoulder, the strong probability was that all the pins would fall in succession, and that he would thus obtain, what is technically known as, "a floorer." Accordingly, Mr. Wilderspin took great pains in aiming his first throw, and when he did aim it well, the pins, by a fixed law of skittles, went down, as the tall gentleman graphically expressed it, "like a shot."

Mr. Wilderspin was one of those generals who could win a battle if his first charge was successful. If he did not succeed in his first charge he generally lost the day. In the mean time, Mr. Wilderspin's friends had been betting upon his throws. The amount, which had begun at shillings, had become sovereigns, and the tall gentleman had lost five pounds in betting against Mr. Wilderspin's throws. As Mr. Wilderspin saw the money in the shape of a crisp bank-note, handed from one to the other, the thought flitted across his mind that he himself ought to reap the benefit of his own skill ; with which he was now greatly elated. He, consequently, ventured a bet or two himself, and in a short time won five pounds. Mr. Wilderspin was averse, on principle, to gambling; and his feeling nature rather experienced pain than pleasure in winning so much of his friends' money. It was therefore, wholly with the design of allowing them to recover what they had lost that he now continued to play and bet rather heavily. He saw that his friends, particularly the tall one, were not nearly his match, and he was therefore anxious to give them every advantage. He was willing to stake ten pounds to one, that his tall friend could not knock all the nine pins down at one throw. The tall gentleman did not seem to think this was giving him much of a chance, and was quite sure he should lose. But fortune which had hitherto been against him, favoured him in this instance. The whole of the nine pins went down like one. Mr. Wilderspin had never seen them go down in

such a magical way. However, he felt somewhat re
lieved in his conscience when he had paid back the
five pounds he had won, and the five pounds extra he
had lost; and would now have ceased to bet, had not
his friends thrown out some insinuations in disparage.
ment of his skill. Having in the mean time, partaken
of some hot rum and water—that compound having
been recommended to him as the best thing to drink on
the top of ale—he was induced to play a three-cornered
game at five pounds a corner. Whether it was that, in
Wilderspin's case, hot rum and water was not the best

WHEN HE IS FAIRLY CLEANED OUT, MR. WILDERSPIN AT LAST GETS A
"FLOORER."

D

thing to drink on the top of ale, or that fortune had
gone against him, it would be hard to say ; but certain
it is that Mr. Wilderspin lost game after game, and five
pounds after five pounds, until he had not another sovereign in his purse.   He had now become desperate and
excited, for he had not only lost his money, but forfeited
his reputation as a player.   He had still one stake left
—his watch.   His friends, who had all at once become
less affable in their manner were ungentlemanly enough
to doubt it being of any value.   Mr. Wilderspin, conscious of having paid twenty pounds for it, indignantly
challenged one of them to refer the question to a
neighbouring pawnbroker.   T. e shorter gentleman
took the watch for this purpose, while Mr. Wilderspin,
with a reeling brain, walked up the board to set the
first pin well for the next throw. Just as he reached
the board, he received a heavy push from behind, and.
from that moment he lost all consciousness until he
was found by the waiter lying among the skittles,
minus his watch, and every farthing of his money.

ADVENTURE THE THIRD.

Mr. Wilderspin is visited by a theatrical friend, who, to his great delight, volunteers to take him "behind the scenes"—Mr Wilderspin is introduced to a great comedian, who introduces him to a celebrated manager.—Mr. Wilderspin being made "free of the theatre," makes a tour of inspection, and though accounting himself rather a *sharp* chap, loses himself among the *flats.*—Is witness of a horrible tragedy, a young lady secretly *executing her pas.*—More *parricide.*—Meets his long lost brother, a "gent" engaged in the house.—Owing to the wonderful likeness, is taken for him by the pantomimic mob, and receives the *compliments of the season.*

I HAVE said that Mr. Wilderspin was a philosopher. He was; and so the loss of his money and the injury to his person were regarded by that gentleman not so much as a calamity as a lesson. Early caligraphical exercises had instilled into Mr. Wilderspin's mind that "Experience teaches." More mature reflection brought Mr. Wilderspin to the admission that teaching was a thing which ought to be paid for. His visit to the skittle-ground with the two gentlemen from the country had taught him that men are not all as they seem, and that confiding natures may be often imposed upon by giving others credit for the same amount of honesty which they possess themselves. Mr. Wilderspin had been taught this valuable lesson, and his loss and his injuries were the price he paid for it. The terms were rather high, perhaps, but the transaction was completed, and there was an end of it. How comfortably we should all get through the world if we were only philosophers like Mr. Wilderspin. How we should be fortified against the ills that flesh is heir to if we could only regard them as blessings. For example, your wife dies, and you are thankful that it is not worse. But perhaps that is not a fair example—not a calamity sufficiently severe. Well; say your aunt dies, and does not leave you her money, as you fully expected and calculated upon. How delightful it would be to be able to sing songs of gladness, to bid your friends wish you joy that you had been delivered from the influence of Mammon! What a refreshing spectacle it would be under such circumstances, to behold a nephew in the longest crape weepers distilling tears of affection over the marble monument which he had erected at his own expense. Mr. Wilderspin was revolving these philosophic reflections in bed one morning, when he received a visit from Mr. Tiverton. Mr. Tiverton was a jaunty man-about-town sort of person, who knew everybody and whom everybody knew in his public haunts ; but who, in his private or domestic relations, was known to nobody. Mr. Wilderspin's good fortune had quickly made him known to many persons of this description. Mr. Tiverton had the *entrée* to various places frequented by public characters, and among others the theatres. Would Mr. Wilderspin like to go "behind the scenes?"

MR. WILDERSPIN IS VISITED BY A THEATRICAL FRIEND.

BEING MADE "FREE OF THE THEATRE" MAKES A TOUR OF INSPECTION.

The very thing above all others which Mr. Wilderspin desired.   He had long aspired to penetrate the
mysteries of the stage, to visit the green room, to see a
rehearsal, to know and be familiar with actors and
actresses.   The most he had ever achieved in this way
was to enjoy the privilege of talking to a clown who
kept a tavern in Long Acre ; but in that situation the
gentleman in question shewed to great disadvantage,
inasmuch as he was not used to the business, and was
prevented by the glass by which he was surrounded,
and the disposition of the persons with whom he had
to deal, from turning somersaults or slapping people in
the face.

Mr. Wilderspin took more than usual pains with his
toilet before proceeding to the theatre, thinking it probable that he might encounter some of the pretty actresses—for Mr. Wilderspin, like all young men who
view theatrical life from the front and by gaslight,
had a settled faith in all actresses being pretty.   The
very word "actress" was associated in his mind with
pink cheeks, glistening eyes, zephyr petticoats, and
handsome legs.   He had not yet had time or opportunity to run this vulgar notion through the percolator of
his philosophic mind, and divest it of the grouts of
conventional error.   Mr. Wilderspin, until this occasion
had never entered the stage door of a theatre.   He had
often wandered backwards and forwards before that
narrow entrance to a popularly imagined broad road
leading to destruction, in the hope of seeing some of

the popular favourites come out or go in ; but the people he had seen were so un-heroic in aspect, so far from being dazzlingly beautiful, and so uniformly (if of the masculine gender) blue and smouchy about the cheeks, that he could never conceive they were the same persons who looked so noble at night.

It must be confessed that, when Mr, Wilderspin did at length realize his long-cherished aspirations of going behind the scenes, he was not so favourably impressed with the aspect of things there as he had expected. The lobby was a dark, dingy, dirty place, reminding him not a little of the view of the Bow Street police-office which the passer-by obtains from the pavement. There was the same row of dirty deal benches, the same barn-door-like wicket, the same cupboard of observation, where the surliest-looking man that could be found was placed, to be a terror to everybody, especially to aspiring dramatic authors who called with their productions to seek interviews with the manager. The only ornaments which relieved the monotony of dirt in this place was a row of fire-buckets, and a couple of notice frames displaying intimations of "a call," and the managerial regulations with respect to the admission of strangers—the latter being a somewhat prolix rendering of the laconic "No admittance except on business," which we see on builders' hoardings. Under the guidance of the privileged Mr. Tiverton, Mr. Wilderspin passed through this outer chamber, and suddenly emerged into a dark labyrinth of steps and stairs, which appeared to have

been specially designed to be the medium of breaking
people's necks. Mr. Wilderspin would certainly have
broken his if the more familiar Tiverton had not taken
him by the hand and called out at the various points of
danger. At length, before he knew where he was,
Mr. Wilderspin found himself upon the stage. The
spectacle was altogether so new and strange to him that
for some moments he stood entranced—not, by any
means, by the beauty or splendour of the scene, but by
its gaunt and dingy wretchedness. Where were the
brilliant colour and cheerful light that made the stage
look so gay from the front? Looking towards the
wings he saw the bare brick walls of the theatre. He
had often seen Macbeth go off at that wing into Dun-
can's chamber ; and he had imagined a royal apartment
there, with a grand canopied couch ; but it seemed that
Macbeth merely went out there to squeeze himself
through between the wing and that dirty brick wall.
Macbeth and other heroes had so often squeezed through
there that the wall near its base had gradually acquired a coat of glossy dirt by way of paint. Casting
his eyes towards the back of the stage, where he had
seen nymphs and fairies bathing in sunlight in Bowers
of Bliss and Palaces of Delight, his vision again encountered bare bricks—bare of everything save a splotch of
paint here and there, where the scenic artists had cleaned
their brushes. Directing his gaze towards the theatrical
skies, he found that those skies consisted of strips of
blue canvas, crumpled, torn, and inconceivably dirty,

MR. WILDERSPIN IS INTRODUCED TO A GREAT COMEDIAN, WHO INTRODUCES HIM TO A CELEBRATED MANAGER.

stretched across from one side to the other like a row
of blue pocket handkerchiefs on a laundress's line.
The machinery, however—the solar system of the
theatrical firmament—was interesting, if not picturesque.
The maze of ropes, pulleys, and cranks was not unsuggestive of the rigging of a ship, and the strange-looking
wooden arms, which, having their shoulder sockets in
the galleries at either side, were raised in all sorts of
menacing attitudes, recalled to Mr. Wilderspin's mind
the arms of the railway signal-posts. The mechanism
of the "flies," so far as it opened up a field for the
pursuit of inquiry and useful knowledge, immediately
aroused in Mr. Wilderspin the greatest curiosity. He
could not, however, resist a feeling of disappointment
at finding the scenes as they appeared from behind so
strongly resembling a ruined sawpit, or an unfinished
house, viewed from the basement story before the floors
are laid. Mr. Wilderspin was quite lost in observation,
when a movement among the wooden arms above him,
and the sudden advance of a pair of flats representing a
watchmaker's shop, warned him that he was in the way.
His friend Tiverton explained that the stage was about
to be set for a dress rehearsal of some of the scenes of
the pantomime. It was not often that they had dress
rehearsals of a pantomime, and Mr. Wilderspin was
fortunate in being present on such an occasion. While
the carpenters were employed in arranging the scene,
Mr. Wilderspin had the pleasure of being introduced to
the leading comic old man, and also to the manager,

both of whom, not having the slightest idea who he
was, but taking it for granted that he was a person to
be recognised and treated civilly, shook him most cor-
dially by the hand. Mr. Wilderspin had never before
been face to face—that he knew of—with a manager
and a comic old man; but now that he enjoyed that
privilege, he could not help thinking that they did not
differ much in appearance from other old fogies he had
met in society. Nor did their conversation give evidence of any great intellectual superiority. The comic
old man—an exceedingly gentlemanly person by the
way—allowed his conversation to run more upon a
roast duck he had had for dinner the day before, than
upon art or literature, while the manager occupied himself in swearing at the carpenters in a manner that rather shocked Mr. Wilderspin, until he discovered that
the epithets he applied to them were used rather as
terms of endearment than otherwise. The setting of
the stage transformed the large open space, in which
Mr. Wilderspin had stood gazing upon the dusky bar-
renness around him, into a perfect labyrinth of avenues
and enclosures. Passing round the first pair of flats, he
completely lost his reckoning; and in a desperate attempt to find an exit, rushed into a recess, where he
came in view of a row of huge masks of aggressive
expression, grinning at him from the floor—a pair of
boots, evidently belonging to a giant fourteen feet high;
a bundle of fairy wands, with golden stars at the end of
them; a heap of theatrical vegetables; and a variety of

IS WITNESS OF A HORRIBLE TRAGEDY—A YOUNG LADY SECRETLY
"EXECUTING HER PAS."

MORE "PARRICIDE

other " properties," the use of which it would have been
difficult to guess at. Taking another turn, he suddenly
came upon the *premiere danseuse*, practising her steps,
in a quiet corner by herself. Her attitude, at the moment of his appearance, being of a repulsive kind, Mr.
Wilderspin took off his hat and hastily withdrew, but
only to encounter a seried front of toes at the back of
the next pair of flats. Though seriously embarrased by
this rapid succession of startling situations, Mr. Wilderspin preserved sufficient presence of mind to hope
that he was not in the way, and that the ladies did not
experience any inconvenience by his untimely intrusion.
The fact was, that the sight of so much limb affected
Mr. Wilderspin with the vague impression that he had
surprised the ladies before they were quite dressed.
Mr. Wilderspin was considerably relieved when the
ladies, suspending their practice, made him a row of
polite curtsies. Mr. Wilderspin here felt that he was
called upon to say something, but not being able to
think of any thing appropriate, he fell back upon that
good hack subject, the weather, and remarked that the
weather was very cold. A chorus of very charming
treble voices replied, "Oh, very cold indeed." At this
moment a lady in a walking dress came up to one of
the prettiest and most youthful-looking of the dancing
girls, and asked her how they were at home? "Oh,
very bad, Miss ; my two youngest are down with the
measles : Johnny has been obliged to go to the hospital
with his leg, and my husband is still out of work."

More conversation passed; but these words made so deep an impression upon Mr. Wilderspin, that he had no ears for what followed. Was it possible, that the young looking, sylph-like girl was the mother of a family? that she who seemed all joy, and grace, and beauty, was the drudge of a sick family? that when she took off that dazzling skirt, clipped off those glittering wings, and washed the pink from her cheeks, she would put on a poor cotton gown and hasten to the bedside of a couple of children pining away and dying in a squalid garret? Yes that was possible—it was true. Mr. Wilderspin now saw what he did not observe before, that the youthful bloom in the girl's cheek was the bloom of the rouge-pot—the brilliancy of her eye, the fire of consuming disease. Ah, thought Mr. Wilderspin, these nymphs of the Palace of Delight do not always bathe in sunshine and feed upon nectar. He had never thought of that; and the young men who go to theatres to see girls dance and act rarely think of that either. If they did, they would not regard them as the mere toys of their amusement, and the fair aim of their coarse jokes and still coarser libertinism.

Mr. Wilderspin was surprised to find, that the lady in the walking-dress was one of the principal actresses of the theatre—a lady whose grace and beauty had long been the talk of the town, and a source of great attraction at the theatre. He did not find her by any means pretty, as she now appeared; nor did he observe any trace of the beguiling smile which she usually wore at night. Out of doors he had heard many scandals about this lady, as he had heard about almost every actress whom he had ever seen or heard of ; but it only required him to step within the theatre to find out that all the stories about her were simply idle and wicked scandals, utterly without foundation. This most virtuous and amiable woman, like many others of her profession, paid the penalty of the stigma which attaches to the stage through the misconduct of a few. When Mr. Wilderspin had become more fully acquainted with the extent of the injustice which respectable actresses suffered through these reckless scandals, it occurred to him to inquire of himself, if society before the curtain were altogether in a position to throw stones at society behind it. On due reflection he came to the conclusion that society, in its present state, was incapacitated from that act of censorious aggression, inasmuch as it had recently, to a considerable extent, adopted glass architecture in the erection of its own residence.

Mr. Wilderspin was suddenly aroused from his reflections by encountering at the wing a gentleman in outward exterior remarkably like himself. This was no other than the "gent" of the pantomime, a personage of recent introduction, whose duty it is to sustain a great deal of ill usage with an equal mind. Mr. Wilderspin had scarcely returned this gentleman's profound bow, when the withdrawal of a pair of flats brought him into the midst of a pantomimic row, where, being taken for the "gent," he was pelted with canvas, carrots, and turnips, and eventually tripped up, by a line

cunningly drawn across the stage by the clown and
pantaloon for the discomfiture of the butcher, the
baker, the candlestick maker, and all the other in-
dustrious members of society, whom it is the mission
of those incurable wags to annoy and bring to grief.
Mr. Wilderspin took this accident in as good humour
as if he had been engaged for the part, and was rather
pleased than otherwise with the experience. He was
not a little amused when the clown told him that he
(the clown) did not discover that he (Mr. Wilderspin)
was not the real gent until he tried to tear his coat up
the back, when he found that he could not do it—the
vestment not being specially adapted by previous dis-
ruption and light tacking together for that purpose.

MEETS HIS LONG LOST BROTHER—A "GENT" ENGAGED IN THE HOUSE.

OWING TO THE WONDERFUL LIKENESS, IS TAKEN FOR HIM BY THE PANTOMIMIC MOB, AND RECEIVES THE "COMPLIMENTS OF THE SEASON."

E

ADVENTURE THE FOURTH.

Mr. Wilderspin having received an invitation from his solicitor, Mr. Scraggs, to take a "bit of Christmas dinner" with the family, gets himself up utterly regardless of expense.—Mr. Wilderspin makes his *debût* in polite society.—Mr. Wilderspin carves, and with decided *eclat*.—After dinner, Mr. Scraggs dilates to his guest on the advantages of matrimony.—Mr. Wilderspin makes himself generally useful.—Mr. Wilderspin pays great attention to Miss Scraggs.—Mr. Scraggs gives Mr. Wilderspin a hint.—Mr. Wilderspin takes it.—After supper Mr. Wilderspin proposes the health of the "lovely and accomplished Miss Scraggs" in a neat (but thick) speech.—Having taken his leave of the family, with the intention of taking a 'bus at the corner, he is discovered taking one in the passage.

ON returning home from the theatre, Mr. Wilderspin found a letter awaiting him. It was from his lawyer, Mr. Scraggs, inviting him to join the family circle of Scraggs at dinner on Christmas day. Mr. Wilderspin's good feeling was continually whispering to him that he was under a debt of gratitude to Mr. Scraggs for having been put by that gentleman in possession of his property. Mr. Wilderspin's logical mind knew better, and would have shut up good feeling in argument with very little trouble. But Mr. Wilderspin, who had the control of both faculties, kept them within proper bounds, and rather inclined to let good feeling have the best of it In fact, Mr. Wilderspin had found out that the exercise.

of the amiable virtues was an excellent preservative of
his self-respect, while it tended to sustain his mind in
that consciousness of right-conduct which is ever a rock
of defence against the assaults of the malignant and the
uncharitable. The *mens conscius recti*, Mr. Wilderspin
was wont to say in after years, when he had acquired
some knowledge of the Latin tongue, is the breastplate
of *æs triplex*, which brings the owner unscathed
through all the dangers which beset him in the battle of
life. Mr. Wilderspin, however, though unwilling to
shake off his sense of gratitude to Mr. Scraggs, could
not feel himself drawn towards that gentleman by any
tie of natural liking. He was therefore by no means
overjoyed on receiving an invitation to dine with him on
Christmas Day. But Christmas Day was at hand, and
he had no other invitation. This reflection brought Mr.
Wilderspin face to face with the fact, that though he
had come into a fortune, he had not yet obtained an entrance into what is called society. With all his means,
he would be as much a homeless waif on Christmas Day
as any poor, penniless wretch who walked the streets.
He could dine sumptuously, it is true, and command the
best of Christmas fare; but it must be at home in soli-
tude at his lodgings, or at some eating-house, where
nobody is seen on Christmas Day save the utterly friend-
less. With old recollections of pleasant Christmas
gatherings under the humble roof-tree of his parents,
Mr. Wilderspin felt that to be rich without the compa-
nionship of friends on Christmas Day was to be poor

E 2

MR. WILDERSPIN HAVING RECEIVED AN INVITATION FROM HIS SOLICITOR, MR.
SCHAGGS, TO TAKE A "BIT OF CHRISTMAS DINNER" WITH THE FAMILY, GETS
HIMSELF UP, UTTERLY REGARDLESS OF EXPENSE.

MR. WILDERSPIN CARVES, AND WITH DECIDED "ECLAT."

MR. WILDERSPIN MAKES HIS "DEBUT" IN POLITE SOCIETY.

indeed. Mr. Wilderspin could not expect much warm friendship from Mr. Scraggs and his family, but he would at least participate in the festivities of the season, and obtain some insight into the manners and etiquette of polite society. Mr. Wilderspin was not ashamed to own to himself that the latter was a desideratum in his case. Perfectly sensible that he was possessed of the innate feelings of a gentleman, he was nevertheless aware that there are many matters of conventional etiquette of which he was ignorant, and Mr. Wilderspin was a man who never despised useful knowledge in any shape. Upon due reflection, therefore, Mr. Wilderspin expressed to Mr. Scraggs, in a neat note, the great pleasure it would afford him to make one of the family party which would assemble round his hospitable board on Christmas Day. It would be useless to conceal from the reader that Mr. Wilderspin about this period furnished himself with copies of the "Complete Letter Writer," and "Hints on Etiquette."

Mr. Wilderspin, having laid to heart Mr. Tipton's maxims about "dress," was by this time fully acquainted with all the mysteries and proprieties of a gentleman's toilet. If he at all transgressed the bounds of decorum it was simply as regards velvet collars and embroidered shirt fronts. In other respects, his dress make-up was unimpeachable. His reception at the suburban villa of Mr. Scraggs was most cordial. The page boy no sooner pronounced the name of "Wilderspin" than the whole family advanced to meet that gentleman with outstretched hands. When I say the whole family, I mean Mr. and Mrs. Scraggs and Miss Scraggs—these constituting the full complement of that branch of the Scraggs' tree. The sole daughter of the house of Scraggs, a young lady of a strong-minded aspect, with a waist of improbable slimness, was presented to Mr. Wilderspin with emphasis, and in due course Mr. Wilderspin had the pleasure of taking that lady down to dinner. Mr. Wilderspin was more struck with Miss Scraggs's conversation than with her beauty, which was not considerable. Though very doubtful if "Hints on Etiquette" would recommend such a topic of conversation with which to engage a young lady, Mr. Wilderspin ventured some remarks upon what he had seen at the Cattle Show. To his great delight and relief, he found that Miss Scraggs was no stranger to agricultural matters. She had read Miss Martineau, and was acquainted with the whole theory of the economy of cow-keeping, even in its most delicate details. The sum of her convictions on this subject was that Somebody's "food for cattle" had effected a great saving in the production of beef. Mr. Wilderspin had reason to believe that it had also a beneficial tendency in the case of the ox, the horse, the sheep, and the pig. During this, and many other conversations on a variety of subjects, Mr. Wilderspin took great pains to follow out the instructions of the "Hints," as to his carriage and deportment. The "Hints" had insisted so much on "carriage," and Mr. Wilderspin had learned his lesson so thoroughly, that he found himself going on as easily as if the carriage he had acquired ran upon wheels. He had practised his bow before the glass at home until he had attained to the most perfect action. On several occasions before dinner he had the opportunity of picking up Miss Scraggs's lace pocket-handkerchief, and the graceful bend and smile with which he presented it to that lady would have done credit to Mr. Brummel himself.

Mr. Wilderspin's stock of accomplishments was in no way overtaxed until dinner time, when being set to carve a turkey—a branch of social science to which he had neglected to give attention—he had the misfortune to encounter a difficulty with a wing, the result of which was that the limb flew off at a tangent, and left its impress on Mr. Scraggs's shirt front. This incident so completely overturned the equilibrium of Mr. Wilderspin's mind, that all the etiquette with which he had primed himself suddenly deserted him, and Miss Scraggs had to make many requests for the salt, and so forth, which Mr. Wilderspin ought to have anticipated. He had settled how he was to request the pleasure of taking wine with that lady, according to the formula laid down in the "Hints;" how, also, he was to ask her mamma to join them; but that little ceremony, and many others which he had arranged to perform at proper intervals, were completely driven out of his mind, until Mr. Scraggs recalled him to a sense of duty by suggesting that no doubt Miss Scraggs would

MR. WILDERSPIN.

AFTER DINNER, MR. SCRAGGS DILATES TO HIS GUEST ON THE ADVANTAGES OF MATRIMONY.

MR. WILDERSPIN MAKES HIMSELF GENERALLY USEFUL.

be happy to take a glass of wine with him, which, of course, only tended to increase Mr. Wilderspin's mortification.   The after reflection which passed through Mr. Wilderspin's mind with regard to this *contre-temp* was, that there is no art or function, however petty, which it is not worth a man's while to learn, since even the inability to carve a turkey may bring destruction to his happiness, and cover him with shame and confusion. When Mr. Wilderspin took to quoting Latin—which was at a period of his life when he discovered that to be supposed to have had a University education was a passport to the consideration of a certain class, which holds that if a man wears good clothes, and can quote Latin, he is *de facto* a gentleman and a scholar, though in reality he may be destitute both of manners and a knowledge of English grammar—when, I say, Mr. Wilderspin took to quoting Latin, he was wont to observe very frequently that *in vino veritas*.   Possibly Mr. Wilderspin was not so much impressed with the truth of this proverb, as he was familiar with its use; for there are many who drag in Latin and Greek quotations into their writings and conversation, not because they are particularly appropriate, but because they are the only ones they know.   However, on this occasion the wine brought out the truth which was hiding in a corner of Mr. Wilderspin's mind.   After a glass or two of Mr. Scraggs's generous sherry, he manfully confessed that he had been very awkward with the turkey, that the accident had very much disconcerted him, and

hoped Miss Scraggs would excuse his want of attention.
This open confession proved good for Mr. Wilderspin's
festive soul, and during the pudding course he had so
far recovered as to be able to combine etiquette with
seasonable facetiousness in a most delightful manner.
Mr. Wilderspin was so much pleased with himself that
he soon began to be pleased with everybody and everything around him. When he found himself *tête-à-tête*
with Mr. Scraggs over a cool bottle of claret after
dinner, receiving a pleasant lecture from that gentleman
on the advantages of matrimony, he had arrived at the
conclusion that he might do worse than act upon his
host's hints—the direction of which were not to be
mistaken—and marry Miss Scraggs. It is much to be
feared that wine, whatever may be its truth-inspiring
qualities, is apt when taken in considerable quantities
to blunt the perceptions of man as regards female loveliness. Mr. Wilderspin's first impression of Miss
Scraggs was not favourable. His natural refinement of
mind would not, perhaps, have permitted him to say
anything harsher of her than that she was plain; but
it is possible that, in an unguarded moment of severity,
he might have pronounced her disagreeable. It is certain, however, that when he returned to the drawing-
room, he was in a condition of mind to regard Miss
Scraggs as rather a pleasant person than otherwise. If
her nose was inclined to be red, that drawback was
counterbalanced by the marble whiteness of her hands.
If her teeth did not emulate the pearls of the ocean,

MR. WILDERSPIN PAYS GREAT ATTENTION TO MISS SCRAGGS.

MR. SCRAGGS GIVES MR. WILDERSPIN A HINT.

MR. WILDERSPIN TAKES IT.

AFTER SUPPER, MR. WILDERSPIN PROPOSES THE HEALTH OF THE "LOVELY AND
ACCOMPLISHED MISS SCRAGGS," IN A NEAT (BUT THICK) SPEECH.

her hair—and it was a decided auburn—was as lux-
uriant as its sea-weed.   Then she had nice arms, and a
recondite arrangement of skirt which betrayed nothing
but a foot of surpassing neatness, which once pressed
Mr. Wilderspin's boot under the table, when that gentleman illuminated the conversational darkness by a
sudden flash of wit.   Mr. Wilderspin's attention to
Miss Scraggs became more and more marked as the
evening wore on, and his confidence having been quite
restored through the influence of her papa's generous
sherry, he was enabled to deport himself according to
the " Hints" with unerring precision.   But alas! confidence is apt to be overweening.   In carrying out that
fundamental principle of politeness, that you should
always bow when offering your services to a lady, Mr.
Wilderspin did not consider that the author of the
"Hints" had not contemplated a gentleman in the act
of "assisting a lady to the kettle," and on accompanying that service with a profound bow, he was suddenly made aware, by a yelp and a scream, that he had
poured about half a pint of boiling water over Miss
Scraggs's pet lap-dog, a mishap which caused Miss
Scraggs to faint, and fall into Mr. Wilderspin's arms,
where she remained for some length of time, rather to
the derangement of that gentleman's graceful deportment—the "Hints" having left him without instruction
as to the course of conduct to be pursued under such
circumstances.   Miss Scraggs, however, was not long
in "coming to."   It was her duty to faint, and she did

faint; but the duty once performed, there was an end
of it. Society demanded so much of her, and it was
not in any way her own interest to carry the thing
further. The incident in no degree changed her conduct towards Mr. Wilderspin, and when that gentleman
sat down beside her, to offer her solace and consolation,
he found her, if possible, in a more amiable humour
than before; while it did not escape his notice that the
lady's parents smiled upon their converse approvingly.
Mr. Wilderspin was so far emboldened by these favourable circumstances, that, on a bunch of mistletoe being
pointed out to him by Mr. Scraggs, he suddenly caught
that gentleman's daughter standing incautiously under
the magic branch and kissed her, a feat which he was
happy to believe caused no displeasure to the young
lady's parents. Mr. Wilderspin was, in the end, so intoxicated with the charms of Miss Scraggs, that he was
prompted, after supper, to propose the health of the
ladies, and to associate the toast with the name of the
lovely and accomplished daughter of their worthy host,
Miss Scraggs, which was drank up-standing, with three-
times-three, and one cheer more for Miss Scraggs—a
proceeding which was scarcely according to the " Hints,"
but which may nevertheless have been warranted by the
occasion, and the lateness of the hour.

When Mr. Wilderspin had taken his leave, Mr. and
Mrs. Scraggs might have been seen at the top of the
stairs, congratulating themselves on the marked attention which their young guest had paid to their daughter.

At the same moment Miss Scraggs might have been observed taking a private survey in the chimney-glass of the charms which had, in the course of the evening, done such terrible execution. Both parties, that is to say the host and hostess and their daughter, followed by the page boy, were hastily summoned from their several occupations to the hall, where, to their great horror and indignation, they discovered Mr. Wilderspin in the act of kissing the servant maid, while receiving from that damsel his coat and hat. Mr. Wilderspin no sooner caught a glimpse of Miss Scraggs and her parents, than he tore open the front door, and precipitately vanished, leaving the innocent abigail to reap the consequences of his imprudence, in the shape of a month's warning from that date, without character.

HAVING TAKEN HIS LEAVE OF THE FAMILY, WITH THE INTENTION OF TAKING A
'BUS AT THE CORNER, HE IS DISCOVERED TAKING ONE IN THE PASSAGE.

ADVENTURE THE FIFTH.

Mr. Wilderspin, under the influence of a new Inverness cape, proceeds to see life in the Haymarket.—Mr. Wilderspin visits the Turkish divan—And enjoys the select society of the saloon.—Mr. Wilderspin visits the Argyle Rooms, and indulges the light fantastic toe.—Mr. Wilderspin, weary of the society of *foreigners* at the Café de la Régence, treats himself to a few natives at Scott's—A gust of wind at the corner of Jermyn street suggests to Mr. Wilderspin that the Inverness Cape would not be a bad sort of thing to fly with.—At a very late hour Mr. Wilderspin is accosted by a "party" of great personal attractions.—At a dark corner he is suddenly made to "remember the garotter," and is *shelled* out.—And finds himself, or rather is found, under the (bull's) eye of the law.—Moral for young men.—Don't shop in the Haymarket after seven o'clock.

THE destinies of mankind are often swayed by the most trifling accidents. A shower of rain may prevent you from going to a party, where, of a certainty, you would have fallen in love with Miss Pepperkin, who, when you had married her, would have brought you an inconveniently large family, and led you a wretched life. O, blessed rain! that dropped thus in gentle mercy from heaven to deliver me from the enthralling blandishments of Miss Pepperkin. A button comes off the front of your shirt just as you are about to rush off to catch the 10.40 express train; you return to have it sewn on, and you arrive at the station just in time to

F

see the 10.40 express move off.   You wait for the next :
when you are half way down the line your course is
impeded by a wreck of carriages, from which the passengers have been extricated, bleeding and bruised—some
of them dead.   This is the train that you were
just one minute too late for.   O blessed female fingers
that neglected to tie a knot at the end of the thread
with which that providential shirt-button was sewn on!
Who shall say what might have been the fate of Mr.
Wilderspin had not his good genius whispered to him
to kiss Mr. Scraggs's servant maid ?   Just imagine what
the consequences might have been had the damsel been
ugly and uninviting!   Next morning's reflection, instead of covering Mr. Wilderspin with shame, brought
solace and consolation to his philosophic mind.   After
what had taken place he could not dare to show his
face at Scraggs's villa again ; and, on reflecting on all
the circumstances (including Miss Scraggs's nose), he
came to the conclusion that all had happened for the
best.   In the true spirit of a philosopher, Mr. Wilderspin extracted a lesson from every incident of his life.
The lesson he extracted from this was—that whatever
amount of truth might be inspired by wine, it was not
safe to make love under its influence ; and this carried
him on to the further reflection, that marriage was not
by any means a step to be taken entirely at the prompt-
ing of the heart, without the intervention of the calmer
judgment of the head, inasmuch as wine, which is capable of making a person see two objects where there is

only one, may as readily make a disagreeable-looking woman appear divinely beautiful. Besides in his more sober moments, Mr. Wilderspin became sensible of the mission he had chalked out for himself. It was not, certainly, to settle down in life before he had seen what life was. Looking into his granary, he found it well stored with sacks of wild oats, which had not yet been sown. He had as yet but opened one sack, and of its contents he had scattered but a mere handful, and those on the thinnest soil. Indeed, it may be said that he had only planted a grain or two in a flower-pot by way of experiment. So Mr. Wilderspin resolved to see life, and sow his wild oats.

"Where was a good place to see life?" he asked of his friend Tiverton.

Mr. Tiverton, understanding by the word "life" the greatest amount of reckless pleasure-seeking amongst the greatest variety of characters, answered "the Haymarket;" and, accordingly, to that peculiar region of the town—for the Haymarket may be said to include more than the street of that name—the two proceeded together.

"The Haymarket," said Mr. Tiverton, as they turned into that thoroughfare, "has killed more men than have been slain in battle since it was, what its name portends, the site of a market for the sale of hay. It is the site of a market for 'chaff' now; and if the skulls of all its victims were piled up in a heap, they would make a mound as large as the great pyramid."

MR. WILDERSPIN, UNDER THE INFLUENCE OF A NEW INVERNESS CAPE, PROCEEDS
TO SEE LIFE IN THE HAYMARKET.

Was Mr. Tiverton speaking literally or allegorically?
Mr. Tiverton was speaking literally.

"Observe," he said, "the peculiar and distinctive
character of this street. Nearly every shop is established
for supplying the wants of revellers. Taverns and cafés
alternate with oyster-shops and cigar divans. Where
is the family grocer, with his good sound Congou at
three-and-eight? Not here. Where those caterers
for the wants of 'home,'—the ironmonger, the uphol-
sterer, the cabinet maker, and the bookseller? If you
seek for these, go to the innocent fields of Tottenham
Court, or the domestic Holborn. As for the Haymarket,
it is the grand emporium for pleasure. There is no
other article kept in stock. Did the grandson of Ha-
roun al Raschid, the great Caliph Vathek, live in these

days, he might find here combined in one the *five Palaces of the Senses*, all ready built and furnished to his hand. Here, at the bottom of the street, is the *Temple of Melody*, or the *Nectar of the Soul*, where, as on the Hill of Pied Horses, are to be found the most skilful musicians of the time. And can you not find here the Palace of the *Delight of the Eyes*, or the *Support of Memory*, where ' statues that seem to be alive, are disposed in a well managed perspective ?' Doth not the Palace of the *Incentive to Pleasure* open a thousand portals to bid you welcome ? Is the *Retreat of Mirth*, or the *Dangerous*, difficult to discover ? Can you avoid the *Eternal* or *Unsatiating Banquet*, where ' the most delicious wines and the choicest cordials flow forth from a hundred fountains that are never exhausted ?' Did you ever read *Vathek ?*" asked Tiverton of his friend.

Mr. Wilderspin had not read that work.

" Well, read it," said Tiverton, " and you will find an exact epitome of the Haymarket pleasure-shops in the Caliph's five palaces. You might fancy sometimes that he was referring to the Casino and the *poses plastique*." Mr. Wilderspin promised to read the work recommended to him, but in the mean time desired to make a personal inspection of some of the Palaces of Delight. The first one he entered was a Cigar Divan, which might appropriately be called the *Palace of Perfumes*, or the *Incentive to Pleasures*. This was a place fitted up with red plush-covered benches and small round marble tables; the walls adorned with gilded mirrors, reflecting and re-reflecting the surrounding objects in so perplexing a manner that it was difficult to say whether the apartment was one or half-a-dozen. One side of the room was occupied by the little marble tables aforesaid, the other by a cigar counter, presided over by a lady in Turkish costume. One thing Mr. Wilderspin noticed as being rather strange, and that was that magnificently dressed women came in by themselves and sat down at the marble tables with all the *nonchalance* of men. They were evidently foreigners, "and no doubt," thought Mr. Wilderspin, "they are simply following the custom of their native country." On ordering a cup of coffee, Mr. Wilderspin was not a little struck by the manner in which a pale-faced waiter juggled with his coffee-pots in filling, or rather half-filling his cup. He was not very sure about the end and object of his performance until he observed that one pot contained coffee and the other hot milk. He could not say that the coffee was better than the decoction with which he had been accustomed to be served at three-halfpence per cup at humble coffee-shops; but as it cost sixpence, and was dispensed by a species of legerdemain, by a French waiter in a white neck-tie, he was willing to believe that it was a superior article. Mr. Wilderspin had no sooner began to sip his coffee and smoke his cigar, than one of the ladies came and sat beside him at his little marble table. There was such an evident intention on the lady's part of making her-

self one of Mr. Wilderspin's party, that that gentleman
was induced to ask her if he might offer her a cup of
coffee. While in the act of addressing her he was in
some doubt lest he might be taking too great a liberty ;
but he was immediately relieved from all fears on that
head by her readily accepting his proffered hospitality.
The lady had no sooner been served with her coffee,
than—putting on a charming smile—she said to Mr.
Wilderspin, "And now I will take a cigarette, if you
please." Mr. Wilderspin was not a little staggered by
this extraordinary request, but on Tiverton nudging
him, and whispering in his ear, "All right!" he went to
the counter, purchased a cigarette, and politely handed
it to his fair companion. "And now," said the lady,
"I will trouble you for a light!" Mr. Wilderspin,
scarcely knowing what he did—for he felt his situation
becoming critical—handed the lady a lighted spill,
which she applied to her cigarette, and immediately
began to smoke with all the ease of an habitual votary
of the weed. The delicate situation in which Mr.
Wilderspin now found himself—seated *tête-a-tête* with
a lady taking her cigar in a public room, almost in
view of the street—so terribly affected his nerves, that
he would certainly have seized the first opportunity to
make his escape, had he not, on looking round,
discovered three or four other ladies smoking. When
he saw the waiters handing them cigars and lights,
and no one appearing to be in any way surprised
at the scene, he perceived that his own particular

MR. WILDERSPIN VISITS THE TURKISH DIVAN.

AND ENJOYS THE SELECT SOCIETY OF THE SALOON.

MR. WILDERSPIN VISITS THE ARGYLE ROOMS, AND INDULGES THE LIGHT FAN-
TASTIC TOE.

friend was only conforming to the habits of the place, and was in no way doing anything *outré* or extraordinary. He could not, however, feel quite at his ease, being haunted by the fear of some one looking in the door and seeing him. What would Mr. Scraggs think if he were to pop his head in? What, Miss Scraggs, when her papa went home and told the family where he had seen Mr. Wilderspin? What would his poor but respectable parents think, if they could only see him? He tried his best to banish these thoughts, and imitate the devil-may-care air of his friend Tiverton but he had not yet become familiar with the manner of sowing wild oats, and his efforts were extremely awkward. He was not sorry, when, having induced his new acquaintance—not without difficulty—to part with him, he got out into the street.

"That is one phase of Haymarket life," said Mr. Tiverton; "but it is a very mild one. Let us see a few more."

The hour of the evening being early—not more than ten o'clock—the life of the Haymarket had not yet got into full swing. "Wait till after twelve," said Mr. Tiverton, "and then you will see some sights." In the mean time Mr. Tiverton took his friend to a tavern frequented by theatrical people, and there in a private parlour he found five or six of the "principals" of a neighbouring theatre, not by any means, in their private clothes, the interesting persons they appeared in slashed doublets and laced boots on the stage. Sir Toby Belch was a fat coarse-looking man, who had more the appearance of a butcher than a son of Thespis and an interpreter of the conceptions of England's immortal bard. Sir Toby drank gin, smoked a long pipe, and utterly eschewed the use of the letter "H." Sir Andrew Aguecheek was a little, pimply, red-nosed old man, who took no particular interest in anything but his brandy and water. Sir Andrew had perfect command of the letter " H," but was in the frequent habit of using it in connection with other letters in a manner not altogether pleasant to unaccustomed ears. Mr. Wilderspin having, in this company, tasted the strong waters of Haymarket life, soon began to drink deep at the intoxicating spring. He went to a neighbouring Casino, and danced polkas and mad galops with his hat on, with ladies in their bonnets and shawls, relieving the monotony of that proceeding by occasional adjournments to a bar, where the ladies invariably preferred champagne to any other refreshment, and where the champagne was charged ten times more per bottle than the juice of gooseberries could possibly be worth in any shape or form. And presently Mr. Wilderspin, following the invariable Harmarket rule, finds himself attempting to quench the fire, that has been kindled within him, by swallowing cool oysters at one of the many establishments where these molluscs are sold. By this time he finds himself what is popularly termed "getting on ;" and feels so relieved of his former embarrassment, and so light and buoyant in spirits, that,

MR. WILDERSPIN, WEARY OF THE SOCIETY OF "FOREIGNERS" AT THE CAFE DE
LA REGENCE, TREATS HIMSELF TO A FEW NATIVES AT SCOTT'S.

A GUST OF WIND AT THE CORNER OF JERMYN STREET. SUGGESTS TO MR. WIL-
DERSPIN THAT THE INVERNESS CAPE WOULD NOT BE A BAD SORT OF THING TO
FLY WITH.

AT A VERY LATE HOUR MR. WILDERSPIN IS ACCOSTED BY A "PARTY" OF GREAT
PERSONAL ATTRACTIONS.

AT A DARK CORNER HE IS SUDDENLY MADE TO "REMEMBER THE GAROTTER,"
AND IS "SHELLED" OUT.

on a gust of wind catching the ample folds of his cape
at the corner of a street, the idea of flight through
space is suggested to him as a probable result of the
rapid process of inflation which is going on within him.
At length, at a very late hour, when he had looked in
at a variety of taverns and coffee houses, at which latter
the tea drank by the frequenters out of china cups was
not unfrequently of pellucid clearness, and at other
times of a peculiar ruby red, he encountered at a quiet
corner a female of great personal attractions and fascinating manners. He had scarcely admitted her to
the privilege of his arm, when he found himself walking
rather unsteadily through a dark court of unknown
latitude ; and before he could make an observation to

AND FINDS HIMSELF, OR RATHER IS FOUND, UNDER THE (BULL'S) EYE OF THE
LAW.

Moral for young men.—Don't shop in the Haymarket after seven
o'clock.

ascertain his whereabouts, he was seized by the throat
by some one behind him, and thrown on the ground,
where he lay in a state of insensibility until a guardian
of the night turned his bull's eye upon him, when he
awoke to a sense of having been half strangled, and at
the same time robbed.

ADVENTURE THE SIXTH.

Mr. Wilderspin has an audience of the manager of the Royal
Amateur Theatre, and selects the part of Richard III. for his
debût.—The manager gives Mr. Wilderspin some hints.—Mr.
Wilderspin orders his costume.—And in the meantime practises
at home.—Mr. Wilderspin's dying scene, and its alarming effect
upon his landlady.—Mr. Wilderspin seizes the opportunity to
practise the scene with Lady Ann.—Her ladyship, conceiving
her lodger to have gone mad, calls in the police, which gives Mr.
Wilderspin the cue to make his great point—" Hoff with 'is 'ed !
So much for Buckingham !"—The tragical tones of Mr. Wilderspin are heard in the middle of the night.—Mr. Wilderspin, in
the tent scene at two o'clock in the morning, "brings down the
house," and " creates a great sensation."

MR. WILDERSPIN'S adventures in the Haymarket had
taught him another lesson, viz : that it was not advis-
able to shop in that quarter of the town after seven
o'clock. A short time after, the following entry might
have been found in his diary :—" I would recommend
this moral to the serious attention of young men generally. Mr. Tiverton scarcely spoke with any exagger-
ation of metaphor, when he said that the Haymarket
had killed more persons than had been slain in war
since the Haymarket was what it now is. The Haymarket has its victims every day—young men dying of
consumption and debilitated constitutions before they
have yet arrived at maturity—older men dragging on

MR. WILDERSPIN HAS AN AUDIENCE OF THE MANAGER OF THE ROYAL AMA-
TEUR THEATRE, AND SELECTS THE PART OF RICHARD III. FOR HIS DEBUT.

THE MANAGER GIVES MR. WILDERSPIN SOME HINTS.

G

a miserable existence, perpetuating their poisoned blood
in an enfeebled posterity—hardened age living in profligacy to the last, tainting the atmosphere of every
society in which they mix. As for the women who
figure in the scene, their fate is often wretched enough,
but they are but the toys of other's pleasures. They
have been made what they are by misfortune. Many
of them would be otherwise if they could ; but the
ruthless profligacy of so-called 'gentlemen,' keeps them
what they are. Our sisters shrink from them as from
something accursed; while they take us—their brothers
—to their arms. Which is the more guilty, the more
worthy of being loathed and despised—we or they?
Truly, the laws of society as respects women have fully
established men as their masters."

It must be confessed, however, that Mr. Wilderspin,
though he was in the habit of setting himself lessons,
and learning them by heart, was very apt to forget
them when any new opportunity opened up of pursuing
his studies in the voluminous Book of Life. His introduction to theatrical society had begotten in his mind
a strong fancy for the stage. He had a great ambition
to don the sock and buskin, and he flattered himself
that he only wanted the opportunity to discover considerable capability for the profession. It was not long
before this opportunity was granted him. Having heard
from Tiverton, that there existed an amateur theatre in
Chapter Street, where, upon payment of a certain sum,
he would be allowed to play any character he might

select, he immediately proceeded to that temple of the drama, and saw Mr. Fitzgilbert, the manager. He found that gentleman—a smouchy person, in a dressing-gown and Turkish cap—occupied with his pupils in the Green-room. The pupils were mostly very young men, with a large expanse of neck, moustaches of most incipient fibre ; young ladies of the ardent temperament, who illustrated their remarks by flouncing at you and striking attitudes, and a few elderly bachelors and maids, who had now taken to acting as they had taken to spirit-rapping and electro-biology, and as they would at some future time take to Ragged Schools and the distribution of Tracts.

On acquainting Mr. Fitzgilbert with his desire to tread the boards, Mr. Wilderspin was informed that the tragedy of *Richard the Third* had been put up, and that several of the characters were still vacant. Richmond was taken, and so were Buckingham, Norfolk, King Henry—indeed, all but Richard, Catesby, and the Lord Mayor of London. Perhaps Mr. Wilderspin would like to assume the principal part, that of Richard himself ; or, if he did not aspire so high, there was Catesby, or the Lord Mayor of London. On reflection, Mr. Wilderspin rejected Catesby and the Lord Mayor of London, as scarcely affording him sufficient scope for the display of his abilities, and eventually chose the part of Richard, for the privilege of playing which he paid the sum of two pounds, that being the

MR. WILDERSPIN ORDERS HIS COSTUME;

AND IN THE MEANTIME PRACTISES AT HOME.

scale price for leading tragedy business. Catesby, or
the Lord Mayor, would have come considerably cheaper,
but, of course, money was not so much an object with
Mr. W. as the desire to win histrionic fame in a prominent part.

The manager of the Theatre Royal, Chapter Street,

MR. WILDERSPIN'S DYING SCENE, AND ITS ALARMING EFFECT UPON HIS LANDLADY.

being anxious that Mr. Wilderspin should acquit himself with credit, advised that gentleman to take a few
lessons in the art before venturing upon a public appearance. Mr. Wilderspin having expressed a wish to
receive instruction, and to pay for the same, Mr. Fitzgilbert at once undertook to act as his master, and gave
him a lesson off hand.

"The great point of the tragedy," said Mr. Fitzgilbert, "is the fight with Richmond. Do that well,
and you will redeem any error or shortcoming that may
have gone before ; and, of course, you cannot forfeit
the credit you may gain in the fight, as after it you have
nothing more to do." Mr. Wilderspin having visited a
costumier, and ordered the handsomest Richard's dress
in his shop, retired to the privacy of his apartments to
practice and study. A little Manual, recommended to
him by Mr. Fitzgilbert, afforded him no slight assistance.
If he wanted to express Love, Grief, Despair, Madness,
Jealousy, Remorse, Rage, Hatred, Revenge, Tyranny,
Villany, and so forth, he had only to turn to the index,
which referred him to the pages where the manner of
depicting these passions was fully described. In Richard,
the ruling passion was, of course, Rage or Anger.
Turning to "Rage or Anger," Mr. Wilderspin was
instructed to represent that emotion, by stretching his
neck out and his head forward, by often nodding and
shaking himself in a menacing manner against the
object of his passion. He was further instructed to

keep his eyes alternately staring and rolling, the eyebrows drawn down over them, and the forehead wrinkled into clouds; the nostrils stretched wide, and every muscle strained; the breast heaving and breath fetched hard; the mouth open, and drawn on each side towards the ears, shewing the teeth in a gnashing posture. Still further, he was enjoined to clench his fist and frequently throw out his arm in a menacing attitude, and, through all, to keep his body in a violent state of agitation. Pulling his trousers up over the tops of his Wellington boots, throwing his cape round his shoulders, and wielding the poker as a sword, Mr. Wilderspin endeavoured to perfect himself in the art of rendering Rage or Anger, by practising one or two of his great scenes before the glass. Whenever he encountered Richmond, he shook himself in a menacing manner at the bed-post, accompanying that action as directed by the *Guide to the Stage*, by keeping his eyes alternately staring and rolling. This he repeated so often, with so much stamping and loud declamation, that his landlady, thinking something serious had happened, rushed into his room in a state of great alarm. At that moment Mr. Wilderspin was in the throes of death on Bosworth Field; but, seizing the opportunity to rehearse the scene with Lady Anne, he rose upon his knees, and addressed the worthy Mrs. Cripps :—

" Nay, do not pause; for I did kill King Henry,
But 'twas thy wondrous beauty did provoke me ;"

Mrs. Cripps wore a wig, and squinted slightly.

> " Or, now dispatch ; 'twas I that stabbed thy Edward,
>   But 'twas thy heavenly face that set me on ;"

Mrs. C. had earned among the lodgers the name of "an old cat."

MR. WILDERSPIN SEIZES THE OPPORTUNITY TO PRACTISE THE SCENE WITH LADY ANNE.

HER LADYSHIP, CONCEIVING HER LODGER TO HAVE GONE MAD, CALLS IN THE POLICE, WHICH GIVES MR. WILDERSPIN THE CUE TO MAKE HIS GREAT POINT. —"HOFF WITH 'IS 'ED! SO MUCH FOR BUCKINGHAM!"

THE TRAGICAL TONES OF MR. WILDERSPIN ARE HEARD IN THE MIDDLE OF THE NIGHT.

"An' I might still persist, so stubborn is
    My temper, to rejoice at what I've done,
    But that thy powerful eyes, as warring seas
    Obey the changes of the moon, have turn'd
    My heart, and made it flow with penitence.
    Take up the sword again (*pointing to poker*) or take up
        me."

Mrs. Cripps, believing that her lodger had gone out
of his mind, conceived him to be a fit and proper person
to be "taken up," and immediately called in a policeman, whose entrance at the very moment when Richard
hears of Buckingham's rebellion, gave Mr. Wilderspin
the cue to make his great point—"Hoff with 'is 'ed !
So much for Buckingham !"

The guardian of the public peace having been made
aware of the nature of Mr. Wilderspin's occupation,
and being satisfied that his violence was not accompanied by any danger to life or property, declared that he
could not interfere ; but, at the same time, expressed
his belief, that it was a case for two doctors, and advised Mrs. Cripps, if he broke out again, to apply for
a warrant to inquire into the state of her lodger's mind.
That lady, however, was induced to give up all immediate intention of following the officer's advice, upon
Mr. Wilderspin promising not to give Richmond so
much trouble in killing him, and to shuffle off his mortal coil a little more quietly.   But Mr. Wilderspin's soul
was in arms and eager for the fray, and though he kept
tolerably quiet for the rest of the day, he could not
resist another tragic burst after the inspiration of his

supper beer. His tragical tones startled Mr. and Mrs.
Cripps from their first sleep, and possessed their minds
with the idea of a burglary, which idea was only dispelled when Mr. Wilderspin, hearing them call for help,
put his head out of his door, and assured them that it
was all right. Mr. Wilderspin was so full of the tragedy
that he could not rest that night. He was continually
waking up to order the instant decapitation of his Grace
the Duke of Buckingham, or to declare that there were
six Richmonds in the field, and that he would give his
kingdom for a horse. A glimmer of moonlight falling
upon Mrs. Cripps's dimity bed-curtains, at two o'clock
in the morning, vividly realized the tent scene to his
fevered imagination, and forgetting entirely that he was
in bed in his lodgings, and not on the field at Bosworth,
he began to rave out the scene at the top of his voice,
which had the effect of waking all the lodgers in the
house, and bringing them all, at the tail of Mr. and
Mrs. Cripps, into his room, to see what was the matter.
On awaking to a consciousness of their presence, Mr.
Wilderspin was inclined to apostrophize them as the
ghosts of Henry, Edward, the Duke of York, and Lady
Anne; but a sudden glimpse of Mrs. Cripps's nightcap
dispelled the illusion, and Mr. Wilderspin took refuge
from the terrible eye of the spectres, by diving under
the clothes, where, on Mr. Cripps having threatened
the embryo tragedian with warning, the spectres left
him to his troubled dreams.

MR. WILDERSPIN IN THE TENT SCENE AT TWO O'CLOCK IN THE MORNING, "BRINGS DOWN THE HOUSE," AND "CREATES A GREAT SENSATION."

MR. WILDERSPIN SEES HIS NAME IN PRINT, AND IS LOST IN ADMIRATION.

ADVENTURE THE SEVENTH.

Mr. Wilderspin sees his name in print, and is lost in admiration.
—Mr. Wilderspin is introduced to Lady Anne.—Mr. Wilderspin rehearses the fight with Richmond.—Mr.Wilderspin invokes
inspiration before a bust of the immortal bard.—Mr. Wilderspin
dresses for the part.—Mr. Wilderspin as Richard III., first plain,
second coloured.—" A horse! a horse! my kingdom for" a pot
of porter.—Mr. Wilderspin theatrically "shuffles off his mortal
coil."—And is greeted at the fall of the curtain as above.

WHEN Mr. Wilderspin first saw his name in print, on a
huge poster, the cup of his ambition nearly ran over.
Here was fame—" Wilderspin to-night, as Richard
III. !" in flaming letters a foot high, and a large con-
course of persons perusing the announcement with the
deepest interest.   On passing one of these posters, Mr.
Wilderspin's attention was attracted to what might be
called a touching incident.   A boy was teaching his
little brother his letters on Mr. Wilderspin's announcement.   The interesting infant knew W and I and L and
D and E and R and S and P and I and N very well;
but experienced some difficulty in pronouncing the
whole word.   When he had got as far as W-I-L—Wil,
D-E-R—der, and appeared to be unable to get any
further, Mr. Wilderspin stooped down and whispered
the word "Wilderspin" in the urchin's ear.

"Wilderspin!" repeated the youngster ; "That's it," said Mr. Wilderspin, "and now there's sixpence for you, my little man." How delightful thought Mr. W., as he walked away to have one's name so popular, that even infants lisp it. Mr. Wilderspin was somewhat disappointed when he was introduced to the Lady Anne, to find that lady of inconveniently large dimensions. He was afraid that the interest of the love-making scene between them would be somewhat marred by the disproportion of their sizes. Certainly the lady's beauty was not so "wondrous," or her face of such "heavenly" aspect, that they could possibly offer any palliation of the crimes which Mr. Wilderspin would have to admit as the results of their influence. It might be said however, that the lady was not at all ill adapted to the task of "taking up" Mr. Wilderspin in a literal sense, or indeed a Richard double his size. It did not tend to reconcile Mr. Wilderspin to Lady Anne, to inform him —as the Lord Mayor of London did in a spiteful whisper—that Lady Anne kept a butcher's shop in Whitechapel, and was troubled with the asthma. Mr. Wilderspin's practice of the fight with Richmond was more satisfactory. As Richmond (a barber's apprentice) himself vaunted, he had a great deal of "fizike." It was Richmond's opinion, that, partly in consequence of this abundance of "fizike," and partly as a natural result of his comprehensive genius, he, Richmond, would make an 'it. The fight, as rehearsed on the clear stage by these two gentlemen, was pronounced by Mr.

MR. WILDERSPIN REHEARSES THE FIGHT WITH RICHMOND.

MR. WILDERSPIN IS INTRODUCED TO LADY ANNE.

MR. WILDERSPIN INVOKES INSPIRATION BEFORE A BUST
OF THE IMMORTAL BARD.

H

Fitzgilbert to be terrific, and "if they only did like that at night, they would bring the house down." As the eventful night approached, Mr. Wilderspin began to be affected by extreme nervousness. He was perfect in the words, perfect in the action, particularly perfect in the fight; but his great anxiety was lest he should lack a proper amount of inspiration. In order to propitiate the "divine afflatus," he made a habit, before going to rehearsal, of intently contemplating a bust of the Immortal Bard, while he essayed to stir up the fire of his soul by inward applications of brandy. It was after one of these exercises, when he had contemplated the lineaments of the Immortal Bard for an unusually long period, and inwardly applied brandy in unusually large quantities, that Mr. Fitzgilbert pronounced his fight with Richmond "terrific."

At length the eventful evening arrived, and Mr. Wilderspin found himself dressing for the part in a state of great trepidation. He had tried on the dress often enough, (having bargained to have it a week beforehand); but now the buttons and buckles slipped from his fingers, and refused to do their office with ominous perversity. One thing he had quite forgotten,—that was the art of making up the face. Luckily he had the *Amateur's Guide* in his pocket. What did it say on the subject? "First wash your face thoroughly." Well, there was no difficulty about that. "Then apply a powder puff all over it." There was not much difficulty about that either, only, when he had applied the powder puff (with rather a heavy hand), Mr. Wilderspin found that he had given himself the complexion of a ghost, rather than that of the dark-visaged monarch he was about to represent. Ah! but that was not all. He was next to "put on, with a hare's foot, a mixture of carmine and Chinese vermillion." When Mr. Wilderspin had followed these instructions with tolerable exactness, his countenance presented a uniform surface of glowing red, which was certainly warlike if nothing else. Turning again to his guide, he read that "if the character to be represented is required to appear with a moustache and whiskers, hair made of crape is next glued to cheeks and upper lip."

Well; certainly Richard would be nothing without a moustache; but Mr. Wilderspin had never thought of such things as crape and glue in connection with that appendage. What was to be done? Was there any mem ber of the company who had sustained a domestic afflic- tion and wore a crape hat-band? Unhappily no son or daughter of Thespis there had recently sustained any such calamity. On applying to one of the three car- penters who worked the scenes, Mr. Wilderspin ob-- tained glue enough to put moustaches on a whole army, and even to stick heads of hair on them if necessary; but what was the use of glue without crape? At length a stray dresser, who had been engaged by Richmond to curl his wig, explained to Mr. Wilderspin that crape hair did not mean hair made of crape, but hair cut i short lengths, and crimped in crape fashion. Havin

MR. WILDERSPIN DRESSES FOR THE PART.

MR. WILDERSPIN AS RICHARD III.—1*d.* PLAIN, AND 2*d.* COLOURED.

"A HORSE! A HORSE! MY KINGDOM FOR "—A POT OF PORTER.

MR. WILDERSPIN THEATRICALLY "SHUFFLES OFF HIS MORTAL COIL."

been provided with a handful of that commodity, **Mr. Wilderspin** was not long in perfecting a very formidable moustache. His only fear was that it might come off when he got warm ; but he was assured that there was no danger of that unless he boiled. When Mr. Wilderspin was completely arrayed, his friend Tiverton, who came to see him, declared that he looked like the coloured edition of Mr. Skelt's great portrait come out of its (window) frame.

There was not a very full house ; but the audience though small, was appreciative. The names of all the actors seemed to be very familiar to the occupants of the pit. Each one as he made his exit was greeted with great applause, and cries of " Bravo Butler," or Jones, or Thompson, as the case might be. Tiverton and Tipton, who occupied front stalls, looked after their friend, and cried " Bravo, Wilderspin !" as loud as any. The play opened very well ; Mr. Wilderspin had got safely over the winter of his discontent, and was fast approaching the summer of a complete success. But alas ! the clouds suddenly began to lower, and dim the brightness of Richard's hopes. King Henry did not know his part, and forgot to take up his cue ; and when Mr. Wilderspin stabbed him to relieve him of his difficulty, in the long speech in the first act, he sternly refused to die ; and had to be stabbed over and over again before he would measure his length upon the stage—a proceeding which caused the audience to indulge in a roar of laughter, and almost knocked all the rest of the play out of Mr. Wilderspin's head. Whether it was that the company generally was embarrassed and made nervous by this incident, or that the actors were wholly imperfect in their parts, is a question that must for ever remain in doubt; but certain it is that from this point every thing went wrong. Lady Anne stuck fast in the middle of her first scene, and resisted all attempts to prompt her. Buckingham and Stanley came on and stood stock still, staring at each other without being able to utter a word ; and, to put the finishing touch to the series of ludicrous mishaps which were by this time convulsing the house with laughter, a strange boy, engaged by Mr. Wilderspin to fetch him some refreshment, suddenly appeared on the stage with a pot of porter. Mr. Wilderspin no sooner observed that his pot bearer was in sight of the audience and causing fresh peals of laughter from boxes, pit and gallery, than he stopped suddenly in the middle of his speech, and, rushing sword in hand at the infatuated urchin, drove him before him to the wing ; making at the same time his own exit before the scene was finished. In the midst of the uproar which followed, the curtain was rung down, and the manager presented himself to beg the indulgence of the audience for imperfections and shortcomings, from which not even the most experienced actors were free, when performing so arduous and difficult a task as the representation of a tragedy in five acts. "With their kind permission they would omit the succeeding three acts, and pre-

sent them with the fifth." This announcement having
been received with great good humour and entire approval, the curtain rose upon Bosworth Field, where
Richard and Richmond met, and engaged in mortal com-
bat with as few preliminary words as possible. The
encounter was terrific in the extreme, and highly ex-
citing. The audience cheered on both the combatants
with cries of "Bravo!" "Well done!" "Go it!" and
their applause only served to urge them to fresh exertions. Mr. Wilderspin quite forgot that it was part of
his business to die. He would not be killed. His
exertions had worked the paint completely off his face,
and even melted the glue which fixed his moustaches.
The thunders of applause from the audience rendered
him deaf to the loudly-expressed hints of the prompter
that "it was time to die!" Richmond whispered in vain
to him, "let me kill you." Mr. Wilderspin heeded
them not, but fought on, and might have continued
fighting much longer had not his moustaches fallen off.
Seeing the two tufts of crape hair lying on the stage,
and finding nothing on his upper lip but glue, he submitted to fate, received Richmond's sword under his
arm, and fell backwards in what would have been a
most effective manner, had not his wig slipped off while
he was falling. It happened, unfortunately, that Mr.
Wilderspin fell a little too near the foot-lights, for on
the green curtain coming down, his feet and a portion
of his legs were left exposed to the audience. Nothing
but this unhappy *contre-temp* could have so suddenly

caused a qualification of the unbounded applause which had been accorded to Mr. Wilderspin all through the fight. That the applause in the end was qualified, and strongly qualified, Mr. Wilderspin himself was painfully sensible ; and it must be confessed that when, on returning home through the rain, he next saw his name in gigantic print, it was not with the same satisfaction that he had first gazed upon it. As Mr. Wilderspin turned into bed that night, he remarked with a sigh—*Ars longa est.*

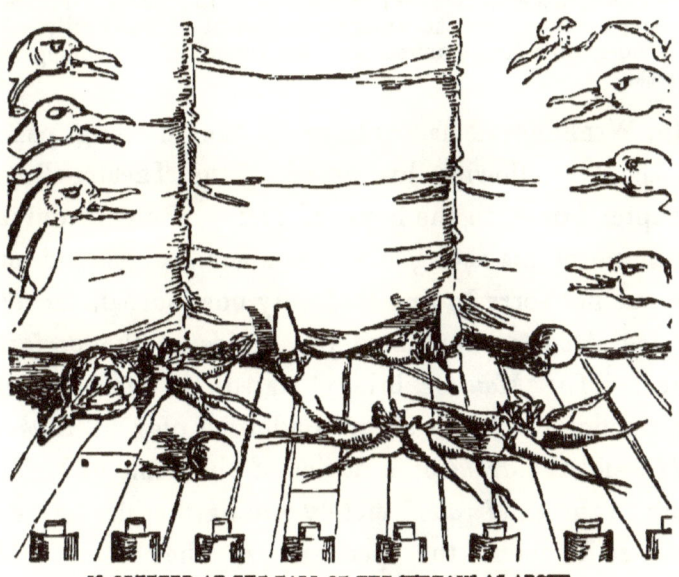

IS GREETED AT THE FALL OF THE CURTAIN AS ABOVE.

ADVENTURE THE EIGHTH.

Mr. Wilderspin buys all the morning papers, to look for criticisms
on his acting.—He looks in vain.—And revenges himself upon
the immortal bard, when Mary Jane announces the arrival of—
Mr. Wilderspin's father!—Mr. Wilderspin's mother!!—Mr.
Wilderspin's brother!!!—Mr. Wilderspin's sister!!!!—Mr.
Wilderspin's aunt!!!!!—The luggage of the family.—Mr. Wilderspin experiences the ardent attachment of his family.—Mr.
Wilderspin's family announces their intention of stopping for a
week.

Mr. Wilderspin had ordered all the morning papers
of the day following his *début* at the Theatre Royal,
Chapter Street, in the hope of seeing some favourable
criticism of his acting. As the affair had turned out,
he was not sorry to find that only one journal, the *Theatrical Monitor*, contained any notice of the performance. The *Monitor* briefly stated the fact of the
production of " Shakspeare's admired play of *Richard
III.*, and the *début* of a novice of the name of Wilderspin in the chief *role*," merely adding that the least that
was said about the performance the better. Mr.
Wilderspin's high hopes were suddenly crushed by this
contemptuous criticism ; but feeling that he had that
within which would come out some day, and astonish
the natives, he did not allow his indignation to carry

nim to any excess beyond that of smashing the sixpenny
bust of the immortal bard, before which he had invoked
inspiration with so little success He had just accomplished this iconoclastic act, when Mary Jane, generally denominated the "slavey," entered to announce
visitors.

Mr. Wilderspin, who was not then in a humour for
company, peremptorily ordered Mary Jane to say he
was not at home—a lie which in a calmer moment he
would have shrunk from imposing upon a fellow creature.

Mary Jane returned unabashed from doing deliberate
iolence to the tenth commandment, and informed Mr.
Wilderspin that the company would wait until his return.

" Who were the company ?"

" Well ; there was an old gentleman, and an old lady,
and a young gentleman, and a young lady, and ——"

Mr. Wilderspin, who thought of the Scraggses,
became alarmed at this catalogue, and commanded Mary
Jane to ask for their cards.   Mary Jane returned to say
that " they hadn't got none."

" Their names ?" demanded Mr. Wilderspin in tragic
tones.   Mary Jane came back with the astounding
intelligence that the name of the whole family was
"Wilderspin."   The hair of Mr. Wilderspin had scarcely
time to stand on head, when there entered unto him in
succession, his venerable father, his respected mother,
his affectionate brother, his ditto sister, and his esteemed
aunt, together with the luggage of the whole family.

MR. WILDERSPIN BUYS ALL THE MORNING PAPERS, TO LOOK FOR CRITICISMS ON
HIS ACTING. HE LOOKS IN VAIN,

AND REVENGES HIMSELF UPON THE IMMORTAL BARD,—WHEN MARY JANE
ANNOUNCES THE ARRIVAL OF

MR WILDERSPIN'S FATHER!   MR. WILDERSPIN'S MOTHER!!

MR. WILDERSPIN'S BROTHER!!!   MR. WILDERSPIN'S SISTER!!!!

MR. WILDERSPIN'S AUNT ! ! ! ! !

It must not be thought, because Mr. Wilderspin manifested surprise and confusion at this sudden inroad of his relatives, that he had been unmindful of them in his prosperity. By no means. He had dutifully communicated his good fortune to them, and had even shared it with them, by sending them both money and presents. His father, who was in the market garden line at Ealing, he had assisted with a hundred pounds, at a time when that gentleman had a heavy bill to make up, and couldn't make it up. His mother he had delighted with a moire antique gown, and a brooch as large as a cheese-plate, which had been a marvel in the eyes of Ealing ever since. His sister he had suddenly helped to assume airs of gentility not germane to the soil of a market garden, by sending her a crinoline petticoat, a cockle-shell bonnet, and a hairy muff. His brother he had set

up as a small capitalist among the juvenile dealers in peg-
tops, rabbits, and clasp knives, with frequent gifts of
five-shilling pieces. His aunt, who had never entertained a high opinion of him, he had brought to regard
him as the hope of the family by conveying to her a
work-box, containing, besides the usual fittings, a hand-
somely bound hymn-book and a ten-pound note. Nor
had he omitted to write to them all dutifully and
affectionately, promising soon to run down and pass a
few weeks in the bosom of the family. In fact, it could
not be urged that Mr. Wilderspin was either a bad son,
a bad brother, or a bad nephew. Mr. Wilderspin's
surprise and confusion arose from the fact that the
pleasure of a visit from his family was totally unex-
pected. The meeting was a most affectionate one.
Father, mother, sister, brother, and aunt flew to their
relative's arms, and overwhelmed him with caresses.
No "long lost brother" of the stage was ever the object
of more ardent attachment. No prodigal son was ever
in more danger of sharing the fate of the fatted calf,
entirely through kindness.

There was only one thought that troubled Mr. Wilderspin. It would be awkward if his family had come
to remain for any time. Shall it be said that Mr. Wilderspin was ashamed of his relatives? Never! He
honoured his father and his mother, loved his brother
and sister, and respected his aunt. But still Mr. Wilderspin could not shut his eyes to the fact that his
relatives, much as he loved them, were not exactly

THE LUGGAGE OF THE FAMILY.

MR. WILDERSPIN EXPERIENCES THE ARDENT ATTACHMENT OF HIS FAMILY.

adapted for the new circle of society in which he himself
now moved. Mr. Wilderspin senior was a worthy, good
old soul, but he *would* wear a bird's eye fogle, and his
hat was chronically of the shocking bad order. This,
to say nothing of his habit of using strong language
and smoking a short black pipe, was a strong reason
against Mr. Wilderspin junior's acknowledging him to
the genteel world in which he moved, as his father.
Feeling, that in his new sphere, manners were more
appreciated than virtue, he encountered the same difficulty with respect to his mother. A more amiable
creature did not exist than Mrs. Wilderspin, but she
was addicted to perriwinkles, which she ate with a pin,
and was wont to pull up the skirts of her moire antique

MR. WILDERSPIN'S FAMILY ANNOUNCE THEIR INTENTION OF STOPPING FOR A
WEEK.

I

to get at a huge dimity pocket, which, for better protection, she suspended by stout cords in the remotest
penetralia of her under-garments. Then his sister,
though temporarily lifted above her station by the pride
of cane hoops and a muff, had a predilection for
twisting her ankles round the bars of chairs, and using
expressions of a streety flavour. For example, on her
brother offering her marmalade for tea, she exclaimed,
"That's your sort ;" and in the next breath pronounced
the condiment "stunning." Her expression of delight
when a cake was brought in took the form of "O,
crikey!" followed by, when she attacked the fifth
slice, "Ain't it jolly, mother?" Master Oliver Wilderspin was not a person to be owned in any society,
owing chiefly to his boots, which were of the unmitigated
hob-nailed order, and his corduroys, which were too
short, deficient of buttons, and unpleasant as to odour.
There would probably have been less objection to Miss
Wilderspin senior (who, when in a state of quiescence,
was simply of limp appearance, like an umbrella that
had been out in the rain, and had been suffered to dry
in a half-closed attitude,) had she not been in the habit,
when asked to partake of liquors, of preferring "a
little neat gin." All these little drawbacks flashing
upon Mr. Wilderspin's mind, in conjunction with the
remembrance of having invited Tiverton, Tipton, and
other friends to spend the evening with him, rendered
him, it must be confessed, decidedly uneasy; and this
uneasiness was increased ten-fold when his attached

relatives announced their intention of stopping a week
with him. The first shock of this announcement over,
Mr. Wilderspin at once recognized his duty to be to put
all other considerations aside for the sake of his relatives ;
and so he wrote to his genteel acquaintances, that family
affairs would prevent him from having the pleasure of
entertaining them for some days. Mr. Wilderspin's
first impression, when he had time to reflect upon his
conduct, was, that in concealing his relatives from his
new circle of friends, he was guilty of an act of paltry
pride and contemptible snobbishness. Practically he
had found himself ashamed of his father and mother,
repudiating his brother and sister, blushing for his
aunt. It was not until his philosophic and reflective
powers had been strengthened by age and experience
that Mr. Wilderspin became sensible of the hollowness
of the indignation with which the world professes to
regard those who, having risen in the world, endeavour
to hide their origin and their unpresentable acquaintances. Is it to honour your father, who is a simple
country farmer, to drag him into so-called genteel
society for people to laugh at him ? Do you show your
love for your honest soul of a mother by setting her up
among fine folks in a drawing-room, where she cannot
find a soul to sympathise with her, and dare not pour
her tea out in the saucer ? If you say that is to honour
and respect your humble parents, then pronounce Mr.
Wilderspin a snob !

ADVENTURE THE NINTH.

Mr. Wilderspin having "passed" his family to their own parish, takes a walk to relieve his feelings.—Stop thief.—The pursuit!— The Thief, Mr. Wilderspin, Tag, Rag, and Bobtail.—Mr. Wilderspin comes in collision with a "buffer," an old one. —Mr. Wilderspin finds himself in an unknown latitude, and is taken by the natives for the Flying Dutchman.—Another party joins in the pursuit—Which brings Mr. Wilderspin to the *tailpiece* of his adventure.

IT would be mere hypocrisy to deny that Mr. Wilderspin felt greatly relieved when he had passed his family back to Ealing. Mr. Wilderspin would not have denied it himself, had he had any congenial friend to whom he could freely impart his feelings on the subject. Still the departure was a great trial to him, in more ways than one. Parting from those we love is always a trial; but when the friends from whom we are about to separate pack their wardrobes in cotton pocket handkerchiefs and blue band-boxes, and carry pattens and fat gingham umbrellas tied together with twine, or an old petticoat string; when this is the case, I say, the ceremony of loading, and getting into, a hack cab at our door, is scarcely pleasant. You and your hack cab, and your departing friends, and their various bundles and packages, are the cynosure of a score of neighbouring eyes. There is a face at every window within view. They watch the bundles and boxes as they come out one by one, speculate upon their contents, and criticise their quality. Then your friends are narrowly inspected. Your father, who is above dress, is pronounced a shabby old man ; your mother, who is holding up her gown out of the mud, gets small credit for her underclothing, because, possibly, she has not put on her embroidered petticoat. Your sister is judged of from her old bonnet and her travelling shawl, and is declared to have little of the appearance of a lady. It is a great trial, a very great trial indeed, this standing at an open door, stowing away your departing friends and their luggage in a cab. I know of no greater trial of the kind, unless it be

MR. WILDERSPIN HAVING "PASSED" HIS FAMILY TO THEIR OWN PARISH
TAKES A WALK TO RELIEVE HIS FEELINGS.

standing to see your furniture packed in an open van when your furniture is very shabby. How you writhe when a deal-topped table is exposed to the gaze of the street. What a shock to your feelings when your bed and bedding are twisted up in a dirty counterpane, with, perhaps, the gridiron or the frying-pan stuck under the fastening! And oh, the ottoman, divested of its chintz, revealing the original egg-box in all its nakedness!

When the cab which carried his family and their fortunes turned the corner of the street, Mr. Wilderspin put on his hat, closed the door behind him, and set forth to relieve his feelings by a solitary ramble. He was wont to observe that he never felt so much alone, or so disposed to philosophical reflection, as in the crowded streets. Many men of great minds have made the same observation ; but there are some great men who cannot even work out a mathematical problem in the recesses of their studies if a barrel organ should be played within six doors of them. But this by the way. Mr. Wilderspin was deep in reflection, and had wandered he scarcely knew whither, when he was suddenly aroused by a cry of "Stop thief!" Turning sharply round, he saw a man running at the top of his speed, and an old gentleman making an absurd attempt to follow him. Without a moment's consideration or reflection, Mr. Wilderspin started off in pursuit. At another time, he would have thought of his dignity and his patent-leather boots, but now he put these considerations entirely aside, and ran through mud and mire

as if his life were on the issue. "Stop thief!" There
is magic in the cry. The windows fly up on every hand;
tradesmen leave their counters and rush to their doors;
the staidest people get excited; the street becomes a
rolling tide of racing humanity, fed by tributary streams
from every alley and turning. In a very few minutes
Mr. Wilderspin found himself running at the head of a
miscellaneous mob of men, women, and children, the
thief being considerably in advance. "Stop thief!"
The cry had been taken up by a hundred voices, and
was now swelling into a chorus. The thief, however,
still kept a-head, presently emerging into a district of
intricate streets. He endeavoured to elude his pursuers
by darting through dark passages and leaping over
barriers. A considerable proportion of the mob had by
this time dropped off, and Mr. Wilderspin soon found
himself almost the only pursuer. His dignity and his
patent-leather boots were now past redemption. On he
went, dashing through pools of water, going splash into
heaps of soft mud, vaulting over the barriers of "No
thoroughfares," never once losing sight of the thief, and
yet not gaining upon him. He had never given himself
credit for such swiftness of foot, and his newly-dis-
covered powers astonished himself no less than the
wondering beings who saw him dart madly by them. At
length the thief, in vaulting over a heap of paviour's
stones, stumbled and came to the ground. Mr. Wilderspin, seizing the favourable opportunity, made a
desperate effort to increase his speed, and was within an

ace of success. He was just making a bound to seize
the man by the skirts of the coat when he slipped his
foot, and fell at full length in the mud. In an instant the
thief was up and away, and another instant Mr. Wilderspin was up and after him. The thief had now evidently

TAG, RAG, AND BOBTAIL.

reached a neighbourhood with which he was well acquainted. In the maze of courts and alleys where the chase now lay, the thief had the advantage of knowing a variety of dark lanes and turnings, to which Mr. Wilderspin was a stranger. For the first time, Mr. Wilderspin lost sight of his quarry, and the inhabitants were neither disposed to direct him, nor to rally to the cry of "Stop thief," which he had just barely breath to utter. Turning a corner sharply at hazard, he had the misfortune to run against an old gentleman, and lay him flat on his back on the pavement. Closing his ears to the cry of "Murder," which this unfortunate individual immediately set up, he ran for some time at random, until, arriving at an alley inhabited by costermongers, he was overjoyed to see the thief emerging at the other end. The costermongers, instead of aiding him in his pursuit, showed a disposition to throw obstacles in his way ; but the impetuosity of Mr. Wilderspin's career was not easily to be checked. The costermongers caught hold of the flying skirts of his cape as he passed them, but the garment slipped through their grasp like a sailstay in a gale of wind. Those vendors of fruit had heard of the Flying Dutchman, and now they were satisfied that in Mr. Wilderspin they had that ubiquitous personage in bodily presence before them. Emerging from the end of the costermonger's alley, Mr. Wilderspin was just in time to see the thief dart down a mews. Notwithstanding that he was beginning to have a stitch in his side, Mr. Wilderspin continued to follow, and down the mews he plunged after him. Here the course of both pursued and pursuer was over manure-heaps, carts, wheelbarrows, and other obstacles; under the bellies of horses that were being rubbed down, through litters of pigs and flocks of geese, and eventually into a forest of clean linen, in the yard of a laundress. Here Mr. Wilderspin was very nearly losing his prey, owing to a wet pair of drawers flapping in his face, and partially depriving him of sight. Just as he emerged from the mews, another "party" joined in the pursuit. The party in question was a ragged white dog, who might have given material aid to Mr. Wilderspin, had he not regarded that gentleman as the person to be caught and detained. This proved very unfortunate, for just as Mr. Wilderspin, on making a last grand effort, got hold of the thief by the tail of the coat, the dog seized him by the skirt of his cape. Now, it happened that Mr. Wilderspin's cape was made of good strong materials, while the coat of the thief was ragged and fragile. Consequently, while the dog held fast to the garment of Mr. Wilderspin the tails of the garment of the thief parted company with the body thereof, and were left in Mr. Wilderspin's hand. Enraged at being baulked of success at the moment it was within his grasp, and feeling it to be useless to remonstrate with his four-footed assailant, he slipped the button of his cape, and left it behind him. Having thus got rid of the dog, Mr. Wilderspin made another grand effort, and was fortunate enough to run the thief into a *cul de sac*. The man ran

THE PURSUIT!—THE THIEF, MR. WILDERSPIN.

MR. WILDERSPIN COMES IN COLLISION WITH A "BUFFER," AN OLD ONE.

MR. WILDERSPIN FINDS HIMSELF IN AN UNKNOWN LATITUDE, AND IS TAKEN BY THE NATIVES FOR THE FLYING DUTCHMAN.

to the end of the court, thinking to find an exit, but meeting with a barrier in a high brick wall, he was fain to place his back against it, and face his pursuer. For some moments Mr. Wilderspin and the man stood panting at each other, unable to utter a word. At length the thief got his breath, and addressing Mr. Wilderspin said—

"Well, now you've got me, what have you to say agen me; come?"

Mr. Wilderspin was scarcely prepared with an answer; but he began to say, "Well you are a thief; and—"

"Stop," said the man, "how do you know that? Have I robbed *you* ?"

Mr. Wilderspin could not say that he had

"Did you see me rob anybody else?"

No, Mr. Wilderspin had not.

"Very well, then," said the man; "what occasion have *you* to hunt me about in this way?"

Mr. Wilderspin was rather posed by this question, and at length said—"Well, upon my word, my friend, I did not think of that before: I don't see why I should hunt you about. There, you are free to pass." And Mr. Wilderspin stood aside, waving his hand to indicate to the man that he might go unmolested.

"Well, thank you; that's something like," said the fellow, walking away leisurely.

"Stop," said Mr. Wilderspin; "I feel that I have persecuted you without due warrant. Are you hungry or thirsty?"

"Both," said the man.

Whereupon Mr. Wilderspin took him into a tavern, and furnished him with a meal of bread and cheese, and a liberal allowance of beer. Mr. Wilderspin talked to him seriously the meanwhile, admonishing him to leave evil courses, and follow a virtuous and honest life. The man was much impressed, and dropped tears of repentance in his beer. Mr. Wilderspin was gratified; and, accompanying the man into the street, by way of giving him the protection of his company, presented him with half-a-crown, and bade him God speed.

Mr. Wilderspin was walking away, big with the consciousness of having done a merciful and Christian act, when it suddenly occurred to him to acquaint himself with the time of day. Feeling for his watch, he found his chain dangling at his side. No doubt he had broken it during the chase. But where was the watch? Gone! Adroitly broken off at the swivel! The truth flashed upon Mr. Wilderspin's mind with the effect of a painful shock. The ungrateful thief, while receiving his mercy and his bounty, had robbed him.

Mr. Wilderspin now saw by what weak logic he had been cajoled into allowing an enemy of society to escape the penalty of his crimes. His watch was gone; his cape lost; his patent leather boots—and, indeed, his whole suit irretrievably ruined. When Mr. Wilderspin had fully reflected upon his folly, the judgment which he pronounced upon himself was — "SERVED ME RIGHT."

ANOTHER PARTY JOINS IN THE PURSUIT;

WHICH BRINGS MR. WILDERSPIN TO THE "TAILPIECE" OF HIS ADVENTURE.

ADVENTURE THE TENTH.

Mr. Wilderspin sets out with a Scottish friend to assist at a "Nicht wi' Burns."—Mr. Wilderspin receives the grasp of friendship.—Mr. Wilderspin having been appointed to serve the "haggis," is rather taken aback by the appearance of that dish, and is in doubt for some moments whether the object before him is a plum pudding, or a terrestrial globe.—Mr. McGab recites an ode to Robbin.—And Mr. McFling performs the Gillie Callum. —"For auld lang syne, my dear"—hiccough—"for auld lang syne, —We'll take a cup of— hiccough," &c.

MONEY, it is written, is " the root of all evil ;" it is " filthy lucre ;" it is " the medium of corruption ;" it " maketh itself wings, and flieth away ;" in fact, a multiplicity of proverbs of undoubted antiquity and high authority pronounce money to be something highly dangerous. There is, we know, a general belief to the contrary ; but how few are the proverbs complimentary to money. "Money makes the mare to go ;"—there's one of some antiquity ; but, upon my word, I don't know another. There is a vast deal of hypocrisy in the world about money. In poetry it is " dross ;" in prose it is " the needful." We all despise and abuse it, yet we are always seeking after it—not always getting it though—and no man considers himself happy if he does not possess it. All this mystification about the true

κ

value of money arises out of that unsolved problem, "What is a pound?" If a pound were not vaguely and generally held to be an *irratamentum malorum*, we might soon get at the true understanding of this question— What is a pound? Say, six good dinners. If I tack myself on to a man who has a sovereign in his pocket, it is not because he possesses a small piece of gold, but because he is enabled to treat me to a good dinner.. If I know another man who has not the command of a good dinner, is it to be expected that I, who care no more for this man than for the other, should laboriously favour him with my society, just to show that I am indifferent to money? Do we put up at a bad inn when we can find accommodation in a good one? Do we prefer tough steaks to tender ones, that we may mortify our teeth in the mastication thereof? Do we court the flavour of a bad egg as a corrective of our hankering after the new-laid article? Is there any more demerit or unworthiness in seeking the company of a man who can make you comfortable with the good things of this life, than in seeking the company of him who simply flatters you, or amuses you with his conversation? When you want to be amused, do you run after a bore? When you want to be fed, do you call upon a person who has nothing in his cupboard?

It was thus that Mr. Wilderspin combatted the arguments of Mr. Tiverton in reference to the large number of friends which began to gather round him when it became known that he was a man of property. Mr.

Tiverton—who, if the truth must be told, wanted to keep Mr. Wilderspin as much as possible to himself—was constantly warning Mr. W. against those persons who were so eager to join his society and court his acquaintance. "Believe me, Wilderspin," Tiverton would say, "they would not be so fond of you if you were poor."

"I shouldn't expect them to be," was Mr. Wilderspin's reply. "Money makes friends, my dear Tiverton ; and I do not find that your own flesh and blood are much warmer in their attachment than those casual acquaintances. The worst calamity that can happen to a man is to die. But how long does your brother mourn for you? How long is it before your widow tosses aside her weeds, and mixes in the gaieties of the world? You, my friend Tiverton, will think of me and mourn me, weeks—months, perhaps, after I am gone. Who will do more? And if I were to fall into poverty, would you not give me a dinner if I wanted one? If I wanted a dinner every day I should become a bore to you ; but, in that case, I should become a bore to the best friend in the world."

Mr. Wilderspin found many friends, and was sought after by many societies. He became a member of various clubs, and was welcome in almost every public resort where he chose to show himself. It was wonderful with what facility people found a qualification for him to enter clubs and societies of a special and specific character. At a literary club he was admitted to be an

author, in virtue of his having written a letter to a
newspaper in defence of poor organ-men. At a dramatic
club he was acknowledged to belong to the histrionic
profession simply because he was a gentleman of property and "a swell." A Scotch acquaintance of the
name of McFling discovered that the Wilderspins were
descended from an old Scottish family of royal blood,
and on the strength of that "fact" procured admission

MR. WILDERSPIN SETS OUT WITH A SCOTTISH FRIEND TO ASSIST AT A "NICUT
WI' BURNS."

for Mr. Wilderspin to the select society of the "Sons

of Scotia." The "Sons of Scotia" were a body whose
society was partly mystic, partly social and convivial,
the balance being in favour of the social and convivial.
It happened when Mr. Wilderspin first made the acquaintance of Mr. McFling, that the birthday of Scotia's
bard, Burns, was about to be celebrated in grand style
by the Society. For the first time in his life Mr.
Wilderspin arrayed himself in highland costume to
attend this ceremonial. Mr. McFling, declared that he
was to the "manner born" in the kilt. If he had any

MR. WILDERSPIN RECEIVES THE "GRASP OF FRIENDSHIP."

doubts about the Wilderspin family being Scotch, they

were completely dispelled by the natural way in which
the Scottish habit sat upon his friend Horatio, the worthy
descendant of that illustrious stock.   Mr. Wilderspin
was gratified by this compliment, but might have felt a
little more worthy of it, if he could have conscientiously
owned that he was quite comfortable with his knees
bare.   Mr. Wilderspin was welcomed by the " Sons of
Scotia" with great warmth.   Each member of the society
came round to extend to him the " grasp of freenship,"
and certainly, if friendship is to be measured by the
ardour and warmth of the grasp, Mr. Wilderspin met
with it then.   Mr. Wilderspin had not been long in the
society of the "Sons of Scotia" before he began to
conceive a high opinion of them.   They seemed to be
all highly intelligent and sensible men — men who
weighed their words, and pronounced them deliberately,
as if they had well revolved their opinions beforehand.
He had been accustomed to hear the Scottish character
disparaged.   He had heard Scotchmen spoken of as
parsimonious, as having no attachment for their native
land once they had left it, and a deal more to the same
damaging purpose.   But here, at least, he saw no evidence of anything of the kind.   These Scots had sub-
scribed a guinea a piece to do honour to their national
bard, and the one theme of their conversation was the
proud supremacy of their country over every country on
the face of the earth.

    " Sur," said Mr. McFling, addressing Mr. Wilderspin,
" we are charged with an aversion to returning to the

land of our birth. It is true that Scotchmen are not apt to return to their native country when they have left it; but, sur, that but proves the cosmopolitan benevolence of the Scottish character. Sur, we are missionaries of ceevelization and enlightenment, who leave our native land to spread the benefits of our industry and enterprise over the wide world." (Great applause from Mr. McGab.) "We do not carry coals to Newcastle, sur; neither do we Scotchmen carry the coals of our ceevelization to where there is a plethora of that article already; but we carry them to benighted lands, which have never been warmed by the fuel of ceevelization. Look round, sur, in this metropolis, and see what the sons of Scotia have done for you. Sur, it was a son of Scotia that established your great national bank. It is a son of Scotia who holds Her Majesty's great seal; to hold which, sur, is the highest trust in the realm. Sur, another son of Scotia, the most dis-tinguished man of the present age, once held that seal. Sur, if I were to go on enumerating all your great men who are sons of Scotia, I should mention the names of almost every man who is noo prominently before the public. Some of them are probably nae immediately connected wi' Scotland, but their forbears were Scotch. Sir, Scotland is a great country, the sons of Scotia are prosperous all over the world; and I am sure, sur, ye winna refuse to drink to Scotia and Scotia's sons?"

Neither Mr. Wilderspin nor any of the sons of Scotia could, of course, refuse to drink the toast, and the latter, it may be mentioned, drank it very much.

MR. WILDERSPIN HAVING BEEN APPOINTED TO SERVE THE "HAGGIS," IS RATHER TAKEN ABACK BY THE APPEARANCE OF THAT DISH, AND IS IN DOUBT FOR SOME MOMENTS WHETHER THE OBJECT BEFORE HIM IS A PLUM PUDDING OR A TERRESTRIAL GLOBE.

MR. MCGAB RECITES AN ODE TO ROBBIN.

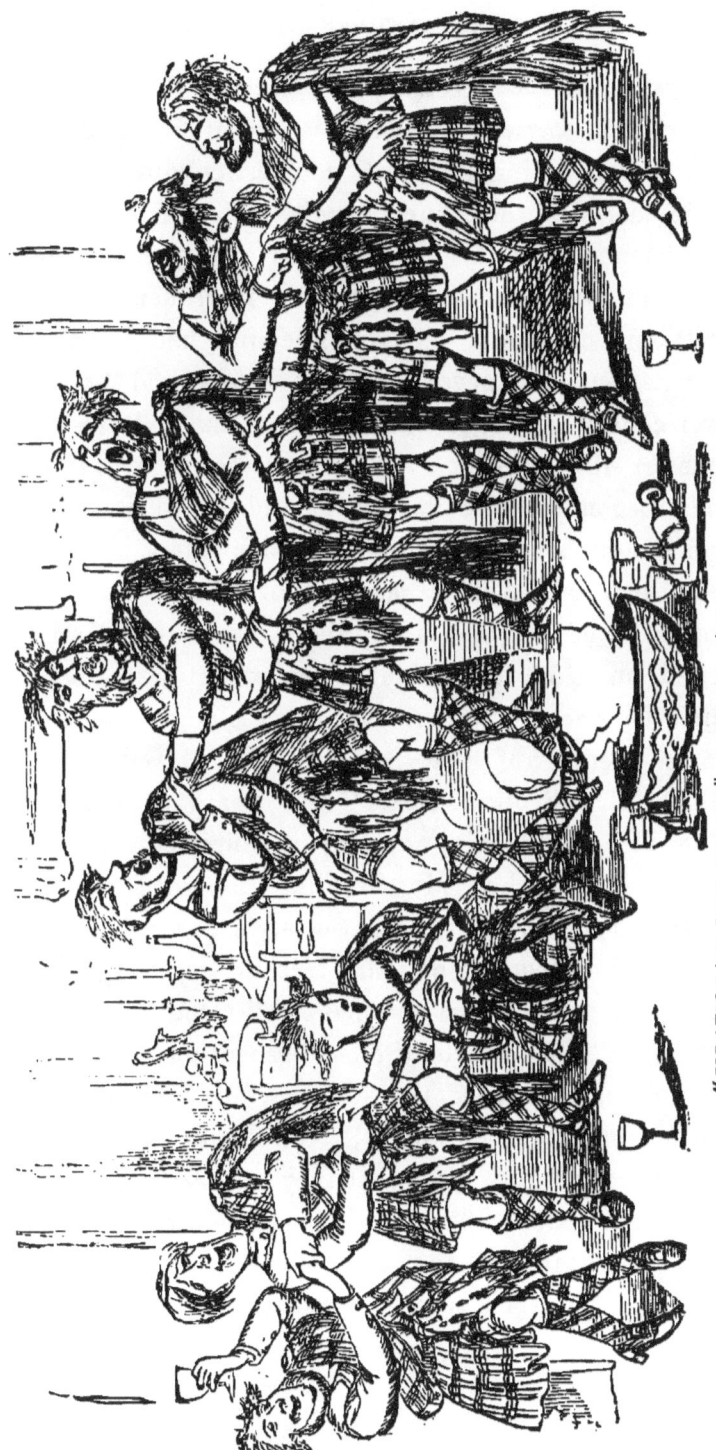

"FOR AULD LANG SYNE, MY DEAR"—HICCOUGH—"FOR AULD LANG SYNE,
WE'LL TAK' A CUP OF—" HICCOUGH, &c.

It will not be necessary to describe the banquet further than to mention, that a variety of Scotch dishes were provided, including, of course, collops, cock-a-leekie, barley broth, and haggis. Mr. Wilderspin's amazement and confusion on being placed before the last mentioned dish caused no little merriment among the "Sons of Scotia." Mr. Wilderspin had heard of a haggis, but had never seen one before, and he had never conceived that it was anything like a terrestrial globe set in a tureen. After the banquet, when the toddy began to take its proper and legitimate effect among the "Sons of Scotia,"—which effect being to make them talk their broadest, and offer each other professions of the greatest love and esteem,—Mr. McGab recited an Ode to Robbie before a bust of the bard, which had been sculptured for the occasion by a talented Scot, a member of that Society. Mr. McGab began with "Hail! Scotia's Bard!" and was very eloquent (if to Mr. Wilderspin not very intelligible) for fully half an hour: when Mr. McFling danced the Gillie Callum, to the music of the Society's piper. As the evening advanced, the national fervour, warming with the consumption of the national toddy, found vent in a variety of vocal efforts, the leading sentiment of which had pointed reference to "coggies," "John Barley-corn," and "Wullie waughs," concerning which last Mr. Wilderspin only knew that they were something to be "taken"—no doubt hot, with sugar. Of course there was a good deal said and sung about "Charlie" and "Johnny," and their respective drums and pipes, both

of which martial musical instruments Mr. McGab
imitated with great felicity. And then there was "For
auld lang syne, my dear, for auld lang syne," when a
great many "cups of kindness" were taken, in obedience
to the injunction of the lyric, leading in the end, when
every Son of Scotia there, including their honoured
guest, was mortal, to the thick and indistinct asseveration
that they "were nae fou, na, nae that fou, but just a
droppie i' their e'e," and a vigorously expressed de-
termination "aye, to taste the barley bree."

It need only be added, that the festivities were kept
up until a very late hour, and that when the Sons of
Scotia dispersed, the neighbouring streets re-echoed for
some time to Johnny's drums and Charlie's pipes, to the
interruption of the pleasant dreams of the denizens
thereabouts.

MR. MCFLING PERFORMS THE GILLIE CALLUM.

ADVENTURE THE ELEVENTH.

Mr. Wilderspin, having adopted a new style of costume, inspires the vulgar boys in the street with the notion of a pump.—And strikes his persecutors, though they are all " under his own size."—Is immediately "struck" in return.—Mr. Wilderspin hails a shower of *rain* with delight, as it gives him an opportunity of being gallant.—For the first time in his life, Mr. Wilderspin tastes the sweets of life.—"The object of interest" takes what Mr. Wilderspin would like to take, a 'bus.—"All right, Bill! there's a case inside!"—Just as Mr. Wilderspin is about to make up to the "party," in the neighbourhood of Turnham Green, he finds himself seriously embarrassed.

MR. WILDERSPIN, when he began to mix in society, saw occasion to reform many of his habits. He found that he had not pitched his style high enough. • He was too much of a gent, and two little of a gentleman. In order broadly to remedy this defect, he changed his style of costume from the somewhat horsey model, which he had first adopted, to the more staid and respectable, yet not slow, clerical fashion then becoming general. The censorship of the street pursued him, of course ; but after a few days of martyrdom, and the occasional assertion of his dignity by an application of his umbrella over the heads of his juvenile tormentors, he was allowed free and unchecked circulation. The long cylindrical coat and the slim umbrella had become too

MR. WILDERSPIN HAVING ADOPTED A NEW STYLE OF COSTUME, INSPIRES THE
VULGAR BOYS IN THE STREET WITH THE NOTION OF A PUMP.

AND STRIKES HIS PERSECUTORS, THOUGH THEY ARE ALL "UNDER HIS OWN
SIZE."

general to excite remark.   Like other fashions which, at
first, appear hideous and ridiculous, it came to be
looked upon as highly becoming ; and young men wondered how they could ever have ventured to appear in
short coats with outside pockets.   There is nothing
more remarkable in social life than the changes which
take place in costume within very short periods.   Five-
and-twenty years ago Mr. Wilderspin would not have
been happy had his coat not been provided with a collar
half a foot high.   In those days the padding and stitch-
ing of the collar was the chief expense of the coat: now
the great object is to have as little collar as possible.
In those days, ladies tied their waists in under their arm-
pits, and wore gigot of mutton sleeves : now the dear
creatures produce a waist effect half down their hips,
and turn the gigot of mutton the reverse way.   Then
the limpness of the female sex was carried to such an
extreme that the contour of the limbs was plainly visi-
ble : now you would be puzzled to imagine a limb at all,
were it not the fashion to show the extremities pretty
extensively.   What odd people our grandfathers and
grandmothers look, as they are depicted in old etchings
by Mr. Cruikshank !   " What odd people our grandfathers and grandmothers look," posterity will say of
us, " as they are depicted in the engravings of Mr.
McConnel !"

On a fine morning in May Mr. Wilderspin, arrayed
in the prevailing fashion, wandered forth into the valley
of life ; and as he strayed by the margin of the Serpen-

IS IMMEDIATELY " STRUCK " IN RETURN.

tine, listening to the ripple of the waters and the songs
of birds, behold there appeared in the distance a maiden
fair to see. Like Irish Molly, she was young and
she was beautiful, the fairest one that Mr. Wilderspin
had seen for many a day. At least Mr. Wilderspin
had no hesitation in inferring as much from a back
view of the lady. She wore a charming little chip bonnet, from under the vallance of which strayed a cluster
of the most lovely auburn curls. Her velvet jacket discovered a waist of fascinating slimness. The skirts of
an extensive sky-blue silk were daintily drawn up by a
" lady's page," disclosing a picturesque red and blue
striped petticoat, from under which peeped a maze of
white embroidery. And oh, the foot and ankle! Mr.
Wilderspin was enchanted,—enthralled. Such a com-
bination of loveliness he had never witnessed before.

MR. WILDERSPIN "HAILS" A SHOWER OF "RAIN" WITH DELIGHT, AS IT GIVES
HIM A CHANCE OF BEING GALLANT.

FOR THE FIRST TIME IN HIS LIFE, MR. WILDERSPIN TASTES THE SWEETS OF LIFE

"THE OBJECT OF INTEREST" TAKES WHAT MR. WILDERSPIN WOULD LIKE TO TAKE, A "BUS."

She was perfectly redolent of sweetness, for as she walked she diffused around an odour of violets. Mr. Wilderspin would have given the world for an excuse to speak to her—to hear the music of her voice—for he was sure her voice was a musical one. But Mr. Wilderspin was no libertine, and his sensitive nature revolted at the bare idea of insulting, or even annoying a lady. How could he find an excuse to address the fair creature? On reflection, he could not satisfy himself that he would be justified in making a remark upon the weather—saying "it was a fine day," for example, or that "it looked like rain." Ha! might he not ask his way —his way to Camberwell, or Islington, or Clerkenwell, or anywhere? No; there was scarcely a colourable pretence for that. A lady in the park was not likely to know; besides, it was a well-known ruse of pickpockets, and he might alarm the lady and bring suspicion on himself. He wished that some wild beast might attack her, that he might slay the animal and rescue her. But there were no wild beasts in Hyde Park. He wished that she might fall into the water, that he might plunge in and bring her all but lifeless body to the shore. But that was a cruel wish; and besides, he couldn't swim, and he hadn't examined his feelings closely enough to be satisfied that he was prepared to die on behalf of the fair maiden. Ha! it is beginning to rain. A brilliant thought strikes Mr. Wilderspin. He will offer her a share of his umbrella. There will be no harm in that—it is an act of simple politeness. He is just elevating his umbrella to advance and say, "Allow me Miss," when the lady is about to emerge from the Park gates. She passes out; crosses the road, and enters a pastrycook's. Mr. Wilderspin hesitates how to act. His excuse is demolished. She is in no need of shelter now. The pastrycook's roof protects her from the inclemency of the weather, and no doubt by this time she is fortifying her inward woman with Bath buns and cherry brandy. Mr. Wilderspin peeps through a row of confectionery glasses, and descries her sitting at a little marble table. He enters, trying to look as unconcerned as possible, and attacks Banburies. Casting a sly glance at the lady at the table, he perceives that his suspicion of cherry brandy was uncharitable—she is washing down her bun with lemonade. Mr. Wilderspin did not, like Lord Byron, object to see women eat. His Dulcinea, as she nibbled her bun, only discovered fresh charms—lips like the ruby; teeth like the pearl. Mr. Wilderspin felt that he could have stopped there and eaten every bun in the shop if the object of his admiration would have remained and permitted him to aid his digestion with a sight of her charms. But just as Mr. Wilderspin had given an order for another Banbury, she rose from her little table—pulled the strings of her "lady's page," to elevate her sky-blue skirt—brushed away the crumbs which adhered to her muff, and left the shop. Mr. Wilderspin followed as soon as his delicacy would permit, and was just in time to see the lady enter an om-

nibus. There was now no time for reflection. He felt
that if he hesitated he was lost : so he hailed the conductor, just as that functionary was giving the signal
to the coachman to drive on, and the next minute was
seated face to face with his inamorata, going he knew
not and cared not whither.

Mr. Wilderspin could now contemplate the charms of
the lady at a convenient distance. He sat and drank at
the fountain of her loveliness until he became perfectly
intoxicated ; so enthralled was he, that he became
oblivious to all that was passing around him. He ceased
to regard the rumbling of the wheels, the jolting of the
vehicle, and the splashing of the rain. There is no
knowing what he might have done had he been a free
agent ; but, luckily, a stout lady kept him firmly em-
bedded between herself and the panel. Presently, when

"ALL RIGHT BILL; THERE'S A CASE INSIDE."

JUST AS MR. WILDERSPIN IS ABOUT TO MAKE UP TO "THE PARTY" IN THE NEIGHBOURHOOD OF TURNHAM GREEN, HE FINDS HIMSELF SERIOUSLY EMBARRASSED.

some of the passengers got out, Mr. Wilderspin by a ruthless effort dug himself up from the obese sides of the dowager (probably leaving his imprint upon her), and placed himself on the opposite seat, next to the object of his adoration ! Now at least there would be no impropriety in addressing her on any of the ordinary topics of the day. It was a common thing for strangers to enter into conversation in an omnibus. It was a privilege which belonged to fellow voyagers in all sorts of conveyances. Mr. Wilderspin had observed and made a note of that; but just as he was clearing his throat to remark to the fair one that " he was happy to see the rain had left off," the lovely creature put forth a dainty little gloved hand, and seized the conductor by the tail of the coat :—" I will get out here," she said, in tones of silvery sweetness. She got out at once, and tripped through the mud to the opposite pavement. Again Mr. Wilderspin's hopes were disappointed. The cup of bliss was dashed from his lips just as he was about to sip. But he was resolved not to be baffled. The omnibus had scarcely moved on when he signalled to the conductor to stop. The lady was still in sight, and he might yet find an opportunity of making her acquaintance. Without waiting for his change, he started off in pursuit. What quarter of the town he was in he could form no idea ; but it was evidently verging upon a suburb. The region of shops had been left behind, and he was now in a district of private villas. It was coming on to rain again. The lady was within twenty yards of him. She might still be at a distance from her home. Surely under such circumstances he would be justified in offering her the protection of his umbrella. Mr. Wilderspin was just about to rush forward and carry this polite attention into effect, when his course was suddenly impeded. A flock of sheep driven hastily round a corner involved him in their midst; and while he was struggling to get free he had the mortification to see his fair enslaver turn a corner and disappear.

Thus, on all occasions, and on every hand, an adverse fate seemed to pursue Mr. Wilderspin through life, dogging his steps, and watching for the best opportunity of defeating his purposes and causing him disappointment and mortification. There were times when the strength of Mr. Wilderspin's philosophy was taxed to the utmost to withstand these rubs of an unkind fortune, and this was one of them. That his philosophy did not give way utterly, and leave him at the mercy of the raging passion within him, can only be attributed to the natural amiability of his character, which enabled him to bear the ills of life with an equal mind.

ADVENTURE THE TWELFTH.

Mr. Wilderspin's *adoration* induces him to watch the "party" to
her *door*. The "party" it will be observed, is occupied with the
knocker, while Mr. W. is occupied with the *belle*—a case of
"knock and ring."—Mr. Wilderspin takes the "party's" number—Mr. Wilderspin consults Jemima, and excites the jealousy
of that active and intelligent officer, Blobbs, 160 P.—Mr. Wilderspin is stigmatized as a libertine by 160 P., and is requested
to *move on.*—Mr. Wilderspin employs the apple-woman at the
corner as his plenipotentiary, and conveys a note to the "party."
—Mr. Wilderspin, as he appeared reading the reply.—The interview—"Party's" big brother and friend in the distance.—Mr.
Wilderspin is required to give "satisfaction."—Mr. McFling
will only be too happy to act as Mr. Wilderspin's second in the
"affair."

IT is an unpleasant thing to get entangled in a flock of
sheep. Mr. Wilderspin found it so. The ewes bumped
him ; the rams butted at him ; the dog barked at him, and
snapped at his coat tails ; and the drover swore at him.
For fully five minutes he was bandied about hither and
thither,—his boots trodden out of all shape by a thousand trotters—his clothes rendered fluffy by shreds of
adhering wool, and his temper ruffled to an extent that
it had never been before. Mr. Wilderspin was not in
the habit of swearing, but he swore then ; and his
curses upon the sheep, the dog, and the drover, were
vented in tones both loud and deep. Here was another

MR. WILDERSPIN'S "ADORATION" INDUCES HIM TO WATCH THE "PARTY" TO HER
DOOR. THE "PARTY" IT WILL BE OBSERVED IS OCCUPIED WITH THE KNOCKER
WHILE MR. W. IS OCCUPIED WITH THE BELLE—A CASE OF "KNOCK AND RING."

MR. WILDERSPIN TAKES THE "PARTY'S" NUMBER.

illustration of those trivial accidents which rule our fate. Perhaps he would never see *her* more. It might have been in the scheme of destiny that he should address her—woo her—win her—make her his wife, and live happily with her ever afterwards. It might have been so ; but his evil fortune had driven up this accursed flock of sheep to cross the path of his happiness, maybe to send him forth into the world to address, woo, and win somebody else who would make his life a misery to him. Mr. Wilderspin had not time to indulge in philosophy just then, or his thoughts might have taken this turn. The moment he escaped from the thrall of those destined muttons, he set off at the top of his speed in the direction which his Dulciana had taken. He ran up one street and down another, athwart squares, round circuses and polygons, and again into open roads, turning right and left, advancing and retreating in the wildest anxiety, but never a glimpse could he catch of that fascinating young creature in the sky-blue dress and chip bonnet. He was almost driven to despair. She was lost to him,—lost to him for ever? Could he ever be happy without her? The sun might continue to shine, but it could never gladden his heart; the birds might warble, but they could raise no response in that desolate bosom. All nature might smile ; but without *her*, Mr. Horatio Wilderspin would preserve a serious front. He was just thinking of sitting down on a door-step, and giving way to a flood of grief, when to his intense joy, he saw his Soul's Delight turn a corner and emerge into the street within a dozen yards of him. He followed her eagerly ; but he had scarcely advanced half a dozen steps before she stopped at a door and knocked. Before Mr. Wilderspin could reach the spot, she had been admitted. There was nothing but the door for Mr. Wilderspin to contemplate. But that was something. A brass plate displayed the name of " Barwise." Then she was Miss Barwise,—no doubt Miss Angelina Barwise. Horrid thought! Could she be *Mrs.* Barwise? Never! But if so, so much the worse for Mr. Barwise. There were two other plates on the door, which enjoined all who might have business at the residence of Barwise to knock and "ring also."

Feeling that he had no "business" to warrant his "admission," Mr. Wilderspin contented himself with taking the number. It was not a lucky number. It was number Thirteen ; and Mr. Wilderspin could not help fancying, as he noted it down, that the lion, from whose jaws depended the knocker, regarded him with a leer which portended mischief. What was to be done now? He could not boldly knock at the door and ask for Miss Barwise—perhaps, Mrs. Barwise ; and the probability of Miss Barwise—perhaps, Mrs. Barwise— coming out again, was, considering the state of the weather, not great. Well: perhaps if he waited about he might catch a glimpse of his fair one at the window. He walked up and down on the opposite side of the way. There was no one at the windows then. Presently, a little grey-headed old man appeared at the middle

window of the first floor. That was no doubt Mr.
Barwise. The age of this gentleman satisfactorily
established in Mr. Wilderspin's mind the improbability
of his being the husband of the young lady in sky
blue. He was Mr. Barwise senior, the father of the
young lady in sky blue—that was clear. Next there
appeared, at the right hand window of the first floor,
an extremely old lady, in a cap of large dimensions.
That was, obviously, Mrs. Barwise, the wife of Mr.
Barwise, and the mother of Miss Barwise. Yet there
was another probability : these Barwises might be the
parents of a youthful Mr. Barwise who was the husband
of the lady in sky blue ! But on reflection Mr. Wilderspin dismissed this suspicion. Young wives were not
apt to reside with their mothers-in-law. After some
time, Mr. Wilderspin's feelings received a shock by the
appearance of a handsome young man at the left hand
window of the first floor. Presently the object of his
adoration appeared beside him, and put her arm round
his waist. Audacious minx ! The handsome youth
took the act in a kindly spirit, and kissed the divine
creature on the cheek. Mr. Wilderspin muttered
" Villain !" through his teeth. The pair were joined
by another young man, with a large beard. The young
lady shook hands with him ; but she did not put her
arm round *his* waist, and *he* did not take the liberty of
kissing her. It was well for Mr. Wilderspin's sanity
that he did not. At length the two young men disappeared from the window, and left the fair one standing

MR. WILDERSPIN CONSULTS JEMIMA, AND EXCITES THE JEALOUSY OF THAT
ACTIVE AND INTELLIGENT OFFICER, BLOBBS, 160 P.

MR. WILDERSPIN IS STIGMATIZED AS A LIBERTINE BY 160 P., AND IS REQUESTED
TO "MOVE ON."

there by herself. Mr. Wilderspin could not help fancying that she saw and recognised him. Yes; she
smiled at him! There was no doubt about it. And
the smile was an approving smile. Was she pointing
him out to her two youthful male friends? No; she
would not do that. Yet Mr. Wilderspin fancied that
he saw her in some such act.

Up and down, up and down, Mr. Wilderspin continued
to saunter, in a high fever of expectancy; but the door
of Barwise never once turned upon its hinges—no one
went in; no one came out. At last, some one. Not
Miss Barwise. No; a neat female "party," in an apron,
with a jug in her hand. The maid going for the beer.
She was not a bashful maid, for when Mr. Wilderspin
smiled at her she smiled in return. Here was an opportunity of learning all about the lady in sky blue—
perhaps of communicating with her.

"Good evening, my dear." It was thus that Mr.
Wilderspin addressed the handmaiden of the House of
Barwise. The handmaiden reiterated the salutation,
and giggled. Mr. Wilderspin, with admirable tact,
produced half-a-crown. "Now tell me," he said,
exhibiting the coin between his finger and thumb, "who
is the lady that came in about half an hour ago?"
"The lady in the Bath chair?" inquired the abigail.

"No; the young lady in sky blue."

"Well; that was——, but come to the corner!"

Mr. Wilderspin went to the corner, and when within
the shadow of the wall, dropped the half-crown into
the abigail's hand, eager to obtain the information.

"Well;" that was"—resumed the maiden—" that was——;" but before she could get out the word, a hand was roughly laid upon Mr. Wilderspin's shoulder. On turning sharply round, Mr. Wilderspin found himself in the grasp of the police.

Mr. Wilderspin, unconscious of any offence against the laws of his country, was about to give vent to his indignation, when the guardian of the public peace gave him to understand that it was not in his public capacity that he interfered with him, but personally, as the acknowledged and encouraged lover of that young woman. On personal and private grounds, therefore, he commanded Mr. Wilderspin to move on. Mr. Wilderspin was about to appeal to the young woman to bear witness on his behalf, when that interesting female threw herself sobbing into the arms of her " regular young man," and appealed for protection ; whereupon 160 P. stigmatized Mr. Wilderspin as a libertine, and waved him off. Mr. Wilderspin retired indignantly, and had the satisfaction to observe the handmaiden bring a pint of beer—no doubt the produce of his half-crown—from the public-house, and hand it to 160 P., under the shadow of " the corner."

Mr. Wilderspin now looked about for another ally ; and soon discovered one, who promised to be both faithful and serviceable, in an old lady who kept a fruit stall.

Did she know the Barwise family ?

" An' did she not ? She had raison to know thim,

MR WILDERSPIN EMPLOYS THE APPLE-WOMAN AT THE CORNER AS HIS
PLENIPOTENTIARY, AND CONVEYS A NOTE TO THE "PARTY."

MR. WILDERSPIN AS HE APPEARED READING THE REPLY.

and respect thim, and be grateful to thim, bless their souls; for a better family, an' one that was more good to the poor, there wasn't in all Turnham Green."

Mr. Wilderspin had no need to ask questions; the old lady was communicative enough. She gave him a catalogue of the family, and all about them, in a breath; but, in her relation, so many of them who were dead were mixed up with those who were living, that Mr. Wilderspin scarcely knew which were the defunct and which the survivors. At last, however, he fixed the old lady to the important fact, that there was a Miss Barwise; that she was young, lovely, and handsome; that her hair was auburn; and that she occasionally wore a sky blue silk dress. This point established, Mr. Wilderspin, with profound knowledge of the world, produced a current coin of the realm of considerable value, at the sight of which the old lady was moved to inform him that she went to the house of Barwise every evening to receive broken victuals from the hands of that charming lady Miss Barwise. She was going there in about half an hour, when she " shut up" for the day. A brilliant thought struck Mr. Wilderspin—

Was Miss Barwise fond of nuts?

She was uncommon fond of nuts; mostly always bought a penn'orth when she passed; and never would take more than six for her penny.

"Good," said Mr. Wilderspin. "Now, will you take half a dozen nuts, which I shall give you, and present them to the young lady when you see her presently?"

As Mr Wilderspin said this, he dropped the coin of the realm into the old lady's palm, and winked.   The old lady grasped the coin, made a feeble attempt to wink in return, and nodded her head.

"Good," said Mr. Wilderspin, furnishing himself with half a dozen of the largest walnuts on the stall, "I shall return in a quarter of an hour."

With that Mr. Wilderspin betook himself to a neighbouring tavern, procured a sheet of note-paper, tore off a small piece, and wrote a note to Miss Barwise, beseeching her to grant him an interview that evening at eight o'clock, under the trees by the toll-gate.   Having written this epistle, he folded the paper up into the smallest compass, and inserted it into the shell of a nut, from which he had carefully scooped the kernel.   With the aid of a little gum, procured from the waiter, he stuck the two halves together, with such neatness, that no one could have discovered that the nut had ever been cracked.   Having accomplished this, he returned to the old lady, and giving her *the* nut, together with five others, enjoined her to present them to the young lady, and try and induce her to crack them in her presence. " If you bring anything in return ——."   Mr. Wilderspin finished the sentence by holding up another coin of the realm.   The old lady repeated her feeble wink, and smiled.

It was almost dark before the old lady appeared at the trysting place, "under the third lamp-post, this side the toll-gate :" but Mr. Wilderspin was rewarded for the suspense he had suffered by receiving from her a little pink three-cornered note. No shop-window being near, Mr. Wilderspin, in his excitement to know the contents, clambered up a lamp-post, and, holding by its iron arm, tore open the pink note, and read—" I will be there. A. B."

The joy which permeated Mr. Wilderspin's frame had the effect of relaxing his muscles so suddenly, that he came down the lamp-post with a run, and so frightened the old lady that she cried out murder. The probability is, that if Mr Wilderspin had not put his hand over her mouth, and given her another coin of the realm, the police would have arrived on the spot and taken him into custody.

At the appointed hour Mr. Wilderspin might have been seen strolling expectantly under the trees of the toll-gate. The clock of the Bar had scarcely struck eight, when he observed a female figure coming towards him. It was she! In the same sky-blue silk, and chip bonnet; in the same neatly-fitting jacket—displaying the same enthralling petticoat, discovering the same bewitching foot and ankle! The only difference was that she was heavily veiled. That was only prudent. Mr. Wilderspin advanced, with an eager step, to offer her his hand and declare his passion. He was encouraged to do so by the smile which t⌣ could detect on the face of the lovely object of his adoration. " My dear Miss Barwise," he began, " my conduct may appear somewhat strange ; but the fire which has been kindled

———." Why did Miss Barwise put her pocket-handkerchief to her mouth and tremble? Was it emotion? or was she giggling? "But the fire that has been kindled," he repeated—

"Must be put out," said a gruff voice at Mr. Wilderspin's elbow.

Looking up in alarm, Mr. Wilderspin found himself in the presence of two tall young men, who stood one

THE INTERVIEW.—"PARTY'S" BIG BROTHER AND FRIEND IN THE DISTANCE.

on each side of him, in a menacing attitude. Almost
at the same moment Miss Barwise ran away, uttering a
cry of—Alarm? Well, no; to Mr. Wilderspin it
sounded rather like smothered laughter; but, that could
not be! Mr. Wilderspin, with his *men sonscius recti*—
that is to say, honourable intentions—indignantly demanded—

" What means this intrusion?"

MR. WILDERSPIN IS REQUIRED TO GIVE SATISFACTION.

" Scoundrel !" said one of the young men.

" Villian !" hissed the other through his teeth, " you shall give me satisfaction. There is my card. I expect yours in return !"

Mr. Wilderspin, utterly taken aback by this proceeding, mechanically presented his card, and received that of his challenger in return.

" And now," said the young man with the beard, (whom Mr. Wilderspin by this time recognised as one of the persons he had seen at the window), "a friend of mine shall wait on you to arrange this matter. Nothing but your blood will satisfy my wounded honour." At these words the two men turned on their heel, and left Mr. Wilderspin standing under the trees in a state of blank stupefaction.

Mr. Wilderspin returned to his home in a state bordering upon distraction. It was some consolation to him to find Mr. McFling waiting in his rooms in expectation of his return. Into his sympathetic ear he poured the whole story of his adventure, nothing extenuating, or setting down aught but that which had actually taken place. At length, when he had exhausted his pitiful tale, he asked Mr. McFling what he ought to do.

" There is but wun thing that you can do, sur."

Mr. Wilderspin anxiously asked what it was.

" As a man of honner-r, sur, you must go out," Mr. McFling replied.

" Go out ?" said Mr. Wilderspin ; " out of the way ?"

"Never-r, sur," said McFling, in determined accents.
"When I say you must go out, I mean that you must
meet the man, and fight him. I have had exper-rience
of these matter-rs in the Peninsula, and I will be your
second. Make your mind easy: I'll arrange everything
for you."

MR. MCFLING WILL ONLY BE TOO HAPPY TO ACT AS MR. WILDERSPIN'S SECOND IN THE "AFFAIR."

ADVENTURE THE THIRTEENTH.

Mr. Wilderspin prepares for the encounter, and, under the guidance of his *Fides Achates*, McFling, practises with the pistol.—Mr. Wilderspin, after burning much powder, and repeatedly endangering the life of the keeper of the shooting gallery, tries his hand at the foils.—Mr. Wilderspin as he appeared on the eve of the fatal day, dictating his last will and testament.—Mr. Wilderspin bids farewell to his landlady and Mary Jane.—Mr. Wilderspin sees the shadow of a coming event.—Mr. McFling endeavours to inspire Mr. Wilderspin with courage.—Mr. Wilderspin proves himself a dead shot.—Fly, Wilderspin! fly!

DUELLING has, in these modern days, been universally condemned as an absurd and irrational practice. Nevertheless, the present writer humbly ventures to think that though the duello originated in a comparatively barbarous age, it was not entirely the offspring of a brutal, or blood-thirsty state of society. In the early times, men, who claimed to be called "gentlemen," were accustomed to regard their honour as something dearer to them than life itself. This maxim, once inculcated, left every man to estimate for himself what constituted a violation of his honour. If he felt his honour wounded by a denial of his assertion, he was as much bound to fight his assailant as if the said assailant had run away with his wife. This was, no doubt, carried to an absurd extreme. Snobs of those days

MR. WILDERSPIN PREPARES FOR THE ENCOUNTER, AND, UNDER THE GUIDANCE OF HIS "FIDUS ACHATES," M'FLING, PRACTISES WITH THE PISTOL.

made a fashion of duelling, just as snobs of these days
make a fashion of being pacific; and practised shots
and swordsmen picked quarrels on purpose to make
a show of their valour in contests where they ran little
risk.   I am not about to defend duelling.   I know that
it is out of place in these days.   The idea of two men
in chimney-pot hats and peg-top trousers going out to
Hampstead Heath to fight a duel is simply ridiculous.
The costume is not picturesque enough for the sort of
thing.   Honour is too cheap for the sort of thing.
How can an age which appropriates the capital of share-
holders, adulterates pickles, and deals in false warrants,
be expected to stand upon its honour?   Honour! The
nineteenth century is out of the article.   But, when
men were chivalrous; when chivalry was a trade to
which boys served their apprenticeship, and men worked
at it as journeymen, it is scarcely to be wondered that
an insult or a slight was regarded as an unpardonable
offence.   In those days, to allow an insult to go un-
punished, was to write your name on the shell of social
degradation.   And what did men do after all, but vindicate what was generally accepted to be their honour?
Do we not still write in our copy-books, "Hold your
honour dearer than your life?"   We all believe in this
theory, but our modern code leaves us no opportunity
of putting it to practical proof; for, having got rid
of honour, of course, the present age is not liable to
be incited to anything of the kind.   When a man runs
way with our wife now, we prosecute him for damages,

and pocket the money. If a villian seduces our
daughter, we sue him for the loss of her services, as
our housemaid or nurse. If a rude fellow calls us a
liar, we say, " You're another !" or throw a tankard at
him. We have nothing now dearer than our life, except
our money. Thus, without saying that duelling is
good, it may be truly asserted that the abolition of the
practice has not left us in possession of a better mode
of vindicating our personal wrongs. A huckster may
be content with damages for his wife's dishonour ; but
a gentleman—in the true sense of the word—is doomed
from that moment to a moral death. His spirit is
mortally wounded ; might he not as well have a bullet
through his body ?

It was by a lecture in this strain that Mr. McFling
endeavoured to reconcile Mr. Wilderspin to a meeting
with his challenger. Mr. W., it must be confessed,
had hinted at giving information to the police, or applying to a magistrate for a peace-warrant; but Mr.
McFling's indignation was vented in such a terrible
manner at the bare suggestion, that Mr. Wilderspin
was heartily ashamed of ever having entertained so
unworthy a thought.

" Prove yourself worthy of your ancestors !" said
Mr. McFling next day, when he had arranged the hostile
meeting. " Remember that all the Wilderspins of
antiquity are looking to you to vindicate the honour
of their illustrious family."

Mr. Wilderspin was, perhaps, more sensible than Mr.

McFling of the vindication which he owed to himself
and "all the Wilderspins of antiquity" in a case of
injury ; but he could not bring himself to feel that he
had been insulted sufficiently to warrant a "life or
death" affair.

"You see," said that gentleman, "I didn't do anything to him ; and he didn't do anything to me particularly, you know."

MR. WILDERSPIN, AFTER BURNING MUCH POWDER, AND REPEATEDLY ENDAN-
GERING THE LIFE OF THE KEEPER OF THE SHOOTING GALLERY, TRIES HIS
HAND AT THE FOILS.

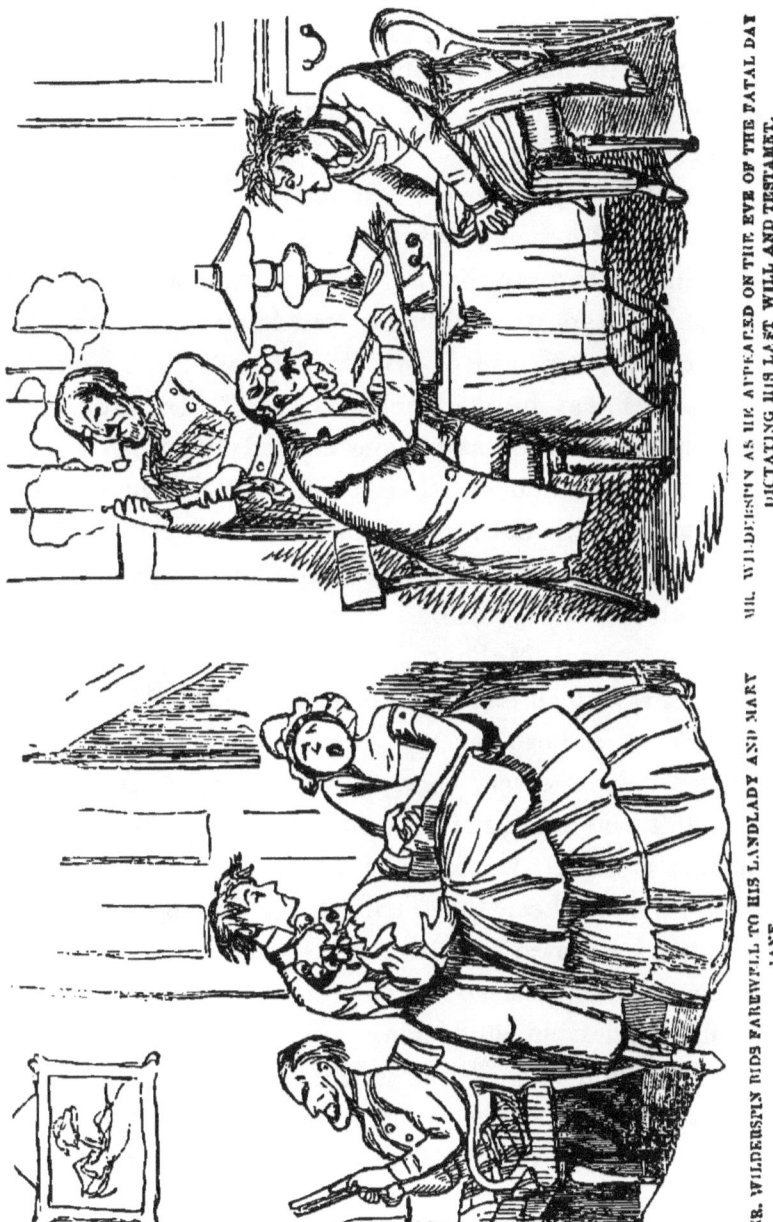

MR. WILDERSPIN AS HE APPEARED ON THE EVE OF THE FATAL DAY DICTATING HIS LAST WILL AND TESTAMET.

MR. WILDERSPIN BIDS FAREWELL TO HIS LANDLADY AND MARY JANE.

" Didn't do anything to you !" exclaimed Mr. McFling, in accents rolling with indignation. " Did he, or did he not, take the young woman away from you ?"

Mr. Wilderspin pleaded that she ran away."

" And did he not come up to you then," pursued Mr. McFling, " and say that he would have your blood—blood ?"   And Mr. McFling repeated that word "blood" in a manner which made Mr. Wilderspin's flesh creep. " When I was in the Peninsula, sur," Mr. McFling continued, " there was a Major O'Grady, who had such a high sense of honour that he would challenge a man for stopping the bottle at the mess.   He would forgive it once ; but if you did it again the Major would have your blood, sur,—blood."

"Oh, please McFling," said Wilderspin, writhing, " don't say blood like that ; it makes me cold."

"That's a mistake, my freen ; it will brace your nerves.   I was a very nervous man in my youth, and couldn't bear the sight of a funeral.   What did I do to cure myself?   I took lodgings at an undertaker's, where I could hear them nailing the coffins day and night.   I got used to it, and at last sang songs to the nailing.   I could sleep in a coffin now."

Mr. Wilderspin shuddered.

" Yes ; and when I was in the Peninsula, I always prepared myself for battle by saying ' Blood and bones ! blood and bones ! blood and bones !' over and over again, to myself.   Expressions, sur, of that forcible order, brace your nerves and relieve your feelings. I knew a parson once, who, when he was vexed, always ran away and shut himself up for five minutes in his study. What do you think he went to his study for?"

Mr. Wilderspin could not imagine.

"Why," said Mr. McFling, "he went to his study to say 'damn.' Being a parson, he could't say it before company, but he said it out loud in his study, where nobody could hear him, and it greatly relieved his feelings."

Having in some degree accustomed Mr. Wilderspin's nerves to the fire of "blood," pronounced with a U and a double D, Mr. McFling took that gentleman to a shooting gallery to practise with the pistol. Mr. Wilderspin was not very familir with the use of that deadly weapon, and his shots went very wide of the mark, owing, as it appeared, to his shutting his eyes and turning away his face, whenever he pulled the trigger. So, after burning much powder, and repeatedly endangering the life of the keeper of the gallery, Mr. Wilderspin came to the conclusion that the pistol was not his weapon. On practising with foils with Mr. McFling, he could not satisfy himself that the sword was his weapon either; and by his friend's advice, he eventually decided to choose pistols; for though it was not probable that he should hit his opponent, the latter might miss him; while with swords, his being run through at the first pass seemed almost a moral certainty.

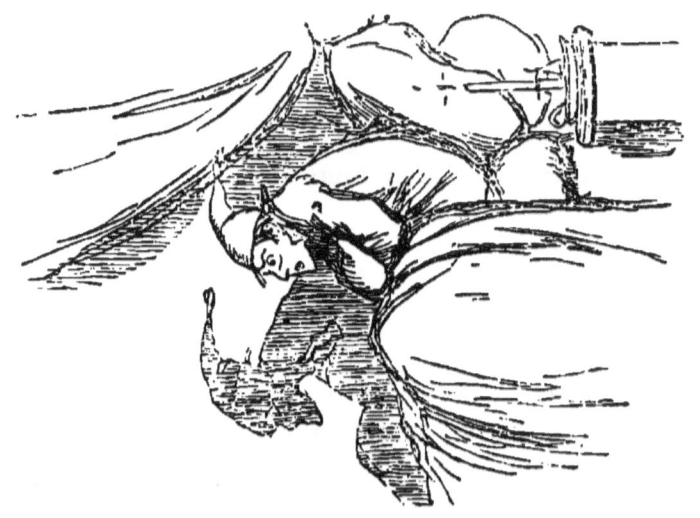

MR. WILDERSPIN SEES THE SHADOW OF A COMING
EVENT.

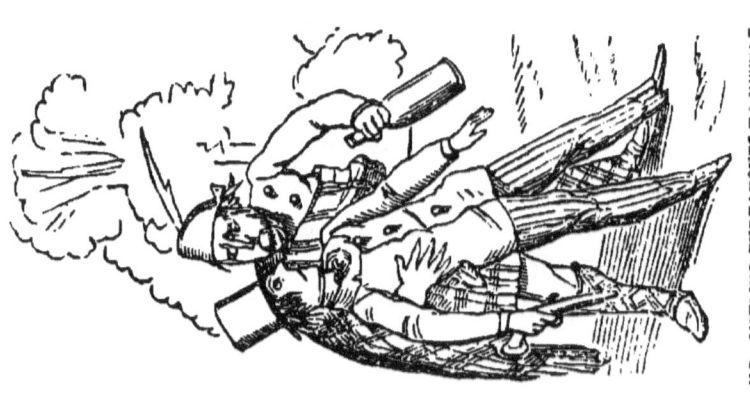

MR. MOFLING ENDEAVOURS TO INSPIRE
MR. WILDERSPIN WITH COURAGE.

The hostile meeting was fixed to take place at an appointed spot on Wormwood Scrubbs at six o'clock in the morning. On the eve of that fatal day Mr. Wilderspin might have been seen sitting in a dejected attitude in his own room, dictating his will to a legal adviser re-

MR. WILDERSPIN PROVES HIMSELF A DEAD SHOT.

N

commended to him by Mr. McFling, while the last-
named gentleman coolly smoked a pipe and loaded the
pistols.   Let a veil be drawn over Mr. Wilderspin's last
will and testament.   Suffice it to say, that it was a dutiful one ; and that while he contemplated a breach of
the Sixth Commandment, he piously and practically
observed the Fifth.   Mr. Wilderspin could not retire to
rest that night without providing against the probable
contingency by taking a solemn farewell of his landlady
and her faithful abigail, Mary Jane.   He was going, he
said, upon a dangerous enterprise, and might never
return ; but he had the satisfaction of knowing that his
rent was paid up, and whatever other charges there
might be, Mr. McFling would discharge.   It is only
due to Mrs. Mivins and Mary Jane to state that they
received this solemn and mysterious communication
with becoming demonstrations of sorrow.   Mrs. Mivins
on receiving a ring from Mr. Wilderspin as a souvenir,
fell upon his shoulder and wept ; while Mary Jane, on
the receipt of a new half-sovereign, gave a sympathetic
howl.   Mr. Wilderspin went to rest, but not to sleep
He tried to say "blood and bones," but the words stuck
in his throat.   Dark omens of evil encountered him
wherever he turned his gaze.   A coal flew out of the
fire with a pop—a coffin !   The candle guttered down
the side and formed a winding-sheet !   Mr. Wilderspin
held his breath in horror, and in the dead silence of
midnight could hear the monotonous ticking of the
death watch.   Starting up suddenly, he found that his

still burning candle had guttered into a cluster of coffins, while the wick had assumed the shape of a funereal plume. And—oh horror!—his own shadow on the wall took the form of a death's head and skeleton!

Mr. McFling arrived before daybreak, and on entering Mr. Wilderspin's apartment, found that gentleman sitting up in bed, looking pale, haggard, and unrefreshed. His last hope had been that something would occur to prevent the duel—that the police would hear of the intended breach of the peace; or that his challenger would make overtures to settle the matter amicably. The countenance of Mr. McFling betrayed no indication of anything of the kind; and Mr. Wilderspin, seeing that there was no escape for him, endeavoured to assume the bravery which he did not possess. When he had dressed, Mr. McFling conducted him to a neighbouring mews, where a cab was waiting to convey them to the place of meeting. It was a cold, damp morning, and not a soul was to be seen in the streets. Mr. Wilderspin's teeth chattered in his head, and a cold perspiration stood upon his forehead. In the gloom which overshadowed the town, every object that met his gaze looked gaunt and spectral. If he withdrew his eyes from outward objects, they fell upon the pistols on the front seat of the cab; or upon the implacable countenance of Mr. McFling. Had a policeman appeared, the probability is, that Mr. Wilderspin would have disgraced his ancient line, by calling upon him for protection; but happily, for the honour of all the Wilder-

spins, no policeman ventured to emerge from the areas
that morning; and the cab, conveying Mr. Wilderspin
and Mr. McFling, rolled on through the streets, and
reached the outskirts before sun-rise.

Mr. McFling thought it prudent to dismiss the
vehicle within half a mile of the appointed spot, lest
the driver should discover their purpose, and give an
alarm.   Poor Wilderspin was by this time in a very nervous condition, and would scarcely have been able to walk
the remaining half mile, had not Mr. McFling prevailed
upon him to swallow some brandy.   When they arrived
on the ground, the mists were clearing off, and the first
rays of the sun beginning to appear on the horizon.   It
was within a few minutes of the hour, and Mr. Wilderspin,
perceiving no one in sight, began to hope that his challenger would not come.   He was beginning to derive
some courage from this anticipation, when two figures
suddenly emerged from a clump of trees and advanced
towards him.   They were his challenger, Mr. Frank
Larkins, and his second, Mr Edward Barwise, brother
of the lovely Miss Barwise, for the love of whom Mr.
Wilderspin was now about to risk his life.   Mr. McFling
at once put himself into communication with Mr. Barwise, and began to measure out the ground.   Twenty
paces was the distance decided on, and the combatants
mutually agreed to fight with pistols.   Mr. McFling
could not refuse Mr. Wilderspin's last request, to make
overtures of peace to Mr. Larkins ; but that gentleman
peremptorily refused any terms.   He had sustained a

gross insult, and nothing but blood would satisfy him. This ultimatum having been given, the combatants were placed, and Mr. McFling advanced to a secure distance to give the signal. Mr. McFling's bandanna had scarcely reached the ground, when, Bang! bang! went the pistols—Mr. Wilderspin's first, that of Mr. Larkins immediately following. Mr. Wilderspin, with his natural repugnance to fire-arms, had turned away his head when drawing the trigger ; but finding that he was not

FLY! WILDERSPIN! FLY!

hit, he ventured to cast his eyes in the direction of his antagonist. Horror! He had shot him—he was lying on the ground, no doubt weltering in his blood. The pistol fell from his hand, and he would have dropped himself, had not Mr. McFling rushed up and urged him to fly.

"Fly! fly!" said Mr. McFling: "justice will be on your track!" And Mr. Wilderspin, being aroused by these words to a sense of his position, turned and fled.

ADVENTURE THE FOURTEENTH.

Mr. Wilderspin, in his flight from justice, meets a countryman, and proposes an exchange of clothes.—The exchange is affected. —Mr. Wilderspin, afraid to confide in the faith of mankind, throws himself upon the hospitality of the brutes.—Shunning the haunts of man, Mr. Wilderspin again appeals to the inferior animals.—Trusting to fate, and his " friend in need," Mr. Wilderspin arrives at the sea-coast.—Mr. Wilderspin trusts himself and "all his fortunes" to the Boulogne boat.—(On his arrival he is narrowly scrutinized by the natives)—Who, regarding him (not wrongly) as a "distinguished foreigner," contend for the honour of his patronage.—Mr. Wilderspin no sooner arrives at his hotel than he discovers from the London papers that the duel was a hoax.—Mr. Wilderspin says " *sacker nom de doo*," and prepares to return to his native land.

MR. WILDERSPIN fled, he knew not whither. From the moment he left the fatal ground he never once looked behind him, but sped onwards, leaving his guidance to fate. The idea of instant pursuit so haunted his mind that he started at every object that appeared suddenly in view. Every breeze that passed him seemed to be laden with the cries of his pursuers. Every person he met seemed to eye him suspiciously. He entered a roadside tavern to obtain some refreshment. While he was sitting there, three men came in one after the other, and looked at him. When he left the tavern, he saw the men standing at the door, gazing after him. At the toll-gate there was a placard pasted

MR. WILDERSPIN, IN HIS FLIGHT FROM JUSTICE, MEETS A COUNTRYMAN, AND
PROPOSES AN EXCHANGE OF CLOTHES.

THE EXCHANGE IS EFFECTED.

MR. WILDERSPIN, AFRAID TO CONFIDE IN THE FAITH OF MANKIND, THROWS HIMSELF UPON THE HOSPITALITY OF THE BRUTES.

SHUNNING THE HAUNTS OF MAN, MR. WILDERSPIN AGAIN APPEALS TO THE INFERIOR ANIMALS.

up, offering a hundred pounds' reward. The word "Murder" was the most prominent one on the sheet; but Mr. Wilderspin lacked courage to read the particulars. He felt satisfied that the reward was offered for his own apprehension, and that the personal description was that of himself. He now struck out from the high road, and wandered through the fields. He had not gone far before he met with a countryman, trudging along with a bundle over his shoulder. For a moment he thought of a detective in disguise; but the broad grin on the countryman's face reassured him, and he ventured to accost him :—

"May I ask if you are looking for anyone?" Mr. Wilderspin anxiously enquired, when he had passed the compliments of the day.

"Well," said the lad, "I be gooing to look for my Molly at the fair."

"Do you want money?" said Mr. Wilderspin.

"Do a want mooney?" said the lad; "that's just what a do wont."

"Then you shall have it," said Mr. Wilderspin, putting a sovereign in his hand. "Now tell me have you any particular fancy for that suit of clothes?"

"Noa," said the lad, "if I can get a better 'un."

"Well, what do you say to mine?" inquired Mr. Wilderspin.

"What do a say? Why, I think I 'ud looked darned smart in that ere quoat at the fair.'

"Well," said Mr. Wilderspin, "will you make an exchange? Put on my suit, and I'll put on yours."

The lad was very much tickled with this idea, but on receiving another sovereign, readily consented; and going with Mr. Wilderspin behind a clump of trees, the exchange was speedily effected. Mr. Wilderspin immediately pursued his journey, leaving the lad to admire himself in his new attire.

Mr. Wilderspin had not walked far before he began to reflect upon the propriety of the means he had taken to elude detection. Had he improved his chances of escape? Clearly not; for now he was still liable to be discovered by his features, while the countryman was almost certain to attract attention by his clothes. By exchanging with the countryman he had left a scent behind him by which he was certain to be traced. Mr. Wilderspin, in his speculative way, had often wondered at the clumsy devices which criminals adopt to elude detection; but now, from his own experience, he could appreciate the obstacles which guilt opposed to reflection and calm deliberation in such circumstances. When he fully realized the double danger in which he had placed himself by the exchange of clothes, he more than ever endeavoured to shun the high road and the haunts of man. He felt that all mankind was his enemy. There was not one of his own species who would not seize and detain him, if he knew that a price was on his head. Nature smiled on him as sweetly as ever. The clouds did not threaten because he had shot Mr. Larkins in fair fight. The sun still shone, the flowers opened their petals, the birds sang

upon the trees, the brooks made music o'er their pebbly
beds ; the brutes did not fly at his approach, or offer to
attack him. Man only was against him. Feeling,
when night came on, that he could not trust mankind,
Mr. Wilderspin threw himself upon the hospitality of
the brutes, and sought a night's refuge in a well-littered
pig stye. An old sow, who, with her progeny, occupied the stye, received him with a grunt of welcome, and
allowed him to lie down in close proximity to her family,
without a motion of protest beyond a curl of her tail,
which Mr. Wilderspin took as a demonstration of favour.
Mr. Wilderspin did not sleep much. He was continually
being arrested and tried, all through the night. The
pig, also, appeared to have troubled dreams—perhaps
she was being caught, killed, and prepared for pork—
all through the night. Mr. Wilderspin and the pig,
however, were of mutual service to each other ; for it
happened, that when Mr. Wilderspin was about to be
condemned to death, the pig gave a grunt and awoke
him ; and when the pig was about to fall a victim to the
knife of the butcher, Mr. Wilderspin started up and
awoke the pig. In this manner, the morning dawned
without any great calamity of dreamland happening to
either.

Mr. Wilderspin thought it prudent not to stay to
breakfast with his host, and at the earliest dawn arose,
patted his porcine friend on the poll, and went on his way.
In passing over a weary common he encountered a donkey, who appeared to be very glad to see him. There

TRUSTING TO FATE, AND HIS "FRIEND IN NEED," MR. WILDERSPIN ARRIVES AT THE SEA-COAST.

MR. WILDERSPIN TRUSTS HIMSELF AND ALL HIS "FORTUNES" TO THE BOULOGNE BOAT.

was no human habitation within view, and it was probable that this donkey had lived a Robinson Crusoe sort
of life for some length of time, and was consequently
not indisposed to make friends, even with one of the
race which it had most reason to dread. It might be
inferred from this, that the donkey is essentially a social
animal, which prefers even to be beaten to being ex-
cluded from the society of mankind. Mr. Wilderspin
again found a friend in the brutes, for the donkey not
only allowed him to mount him, but immediately trotted
off in the direction which Mr. Wilderspin had been pursuing. From the bare and undulating appearance of the
country around him, Mr. Wilderspin now became sensible that he was rapidly approaching the sea. Just as
the sun was setting, his four-footed friend brought him
to the top of a hill from which he could command a
view of the ocean, and a seaport at a little distance to
the right. Mr. Wilderspin here dismounted, and treating his friend to some crumbs of biscuit which he had
got in his bundle, embraced him, and turned his head
in the direction whence he had come. For a moment,
Mr. Wilderspin and the donkey stood gazing at each
other with regretful looks. The next they turned their
backs upon each other, and each sorrowfully pursued
his way.

Having arrived at the seaport, Mr. Wilderspin ascer-
tained that a boat was about to sail that evening for
Boulogne. He at once resolved to put himself on board,
and take farewell of his native land. This would have

been easy enough if there had been nothing to do but pay the fare, for Mr. Wilderspin had still abundant funds; but, unfortunately, a passport was necessary; and a Consul was just one of those persons whom Mr. Wilderspin was most anxious to avoid. As he was sitting over the fire in an obscure tavern, thinking what course to pursue, a man dressed like a Frenchman entered and accosted him. He had seen him previously in the bar, when he was making inquiries about the starting of the steamer and the passport regulations. Presently the man drew up close to where Mr. Wilderspin sat, and half-whispered in his ear—

"Do you wish to go to France?"

Mr. Wilderspin said, "Yes."

"You want a passport?"

"I do."

"Have you got money?"

"I have."

"Would you like a better suit of clothes than that you have on? I ask because I should like yours?"

Mr. Wilderspin now understood his new acquaintance: he was a brother in misfortune—perhaps an unfortunate duellist like himself. Mr. Wilderspin did not stay to ask questions, but speedily made the exchange; and, fortunately, it happened that he and his friend were very much alike, so that the description in the passport tallied with his own appearance as nearly as possible. Mr. Wilderspin now put himself on board the Boulogne boat, and in a very short time might have been seen

ON HIS ARRIVAL HE IS NARROWLY SCRUTINIZED BY THE NATIVES, WHO, REGARD-
ING HIM (NOT WRONGLY) AS A "DISTINGUISHED FOREIGNER," CONTEND FOR
THE HONOUR OF HIS PATRONAGE.

MR. WILDERSPIN NO SOONER ARRIVES AT HIS HOTEL, THAN HE DISCOVERS FROM
THE LONDON PAPERS THAT THE DUEL WAS A HOAX. MR WILDERSPIN SAYS
"SACKER NOM DE DOO," AND PREPARES TO RETURN TO HIS NATIVE LAND.

sacrificing to Neptune with much devotion. On his arrival at Boulogne, Mr. Wilderspin found himself an object of great interest to the natives. There was great contention among them for the honour of his patronage. The names of a hundred hotels were balled in his ears as he passed along the quay, and rival *commissionaires* threatened to dismember him and distribute him in limbs and joints over all the hotels in the place.

After a desperate struggle, Mr. Wilderspin was carried off in triumph by the bravest and strongest of the *commissionaires*, who actually floored his rivals in order to secure the prize. Once within doors, Mr. Wilderspin was not long in retiring to rest, and, for the first time since he fled from Wormwood Scrubbs, he slept soundly. The morning, however, awoke him to a sense of his awful position, and he suffered a high fever of excitement until the arrival of the London papers. When the *Times* was put into his hand, he scarcely dared to open it : he dreaded to see a record of the terrible affair in which he had been engaged, with perhaps, a description of his appearance, and the offer of a reward for his apprehension. At length he summoned up nerve to open the paper. Almost the first paragraph upon which his eye lighted, was as follows :—

" A DUEL ON WORMWOOD SCRUBBS. — A hostile meeting took place yesterday morning between two gentlemen—one of whom is pretty well known for his eccentricity—the result being the supposed death of the eccentric gentleman's opponent. The fact seems to be that the latter played off a hoax upon the eccentric gentleman, and pretended to fall dead when he fired his pistol. The best of the joke—if joke it can be called is that the eccentric gentleman has fled the country, in the belief that he actually killed his opponent."

On reading this paragraph, Mr. Wilderspin swore a French oath, paid his bill at the hotel, and made all haste back to his native land.

ADVENTURE THE FIFTEENTH.

Mr. Wilderspin receives a deputation from the inhabitants of his native Pumpington, who invite him to stand for the borough.— Mr. Wilderspin is drawn through his native town in triumph.— Mr. Wilderspin endeavours to ingratiate himself with the constituency in the approved fashion.—Mr. Wilderspin makes a little arrangement with a tavern keeper—a case of the Publican and the Sinner.—Mr. Wilderspin addresses his constituents.— Mr. Wilderspin is assailed by the supporters of the bloated aristocrat, the candidate in opposition.—But eventually obtains a show of (rather dirty) hands. N.B. Wilderspin's Central Committee Room, 158, Fleet Street. Vote for Wilderspin!

IT was not long after the affair at Wormwood Scrubbs, that Mr. Wilderspin, as the result of much cogitation and reflection, arrived at the conclusion that he had not pitched himself quite high enough in the scale of society. The clubs to which he belonged were held at taverns, and were all more or less devoted to the worship of Bacchus. It is true that the devotion of the worshippers was as ardent as need be, but the libations poured upon the altar were of the humblest class. Then his friends and companions, though persons of eminent social qualities, and high intellectual powers, were not in outward aspect, in habits, or in manners calculated to bestow much lustre upon those who associated with them. And Mr. Wilderspin soon began to find out that he was not strong enough to shine by his own light in such society. He felt himself to be a satellite wandering about the social firmament in search of a sun to shine upon and illuminate him. It was true that in a small sphere he derived a slight halo of glory from being privileged to walk arm-in-arm with a celebrated actor, author, or artist; but these gentlemen were so much accustomed to set the observances of society at defiance, that, in the end, Mr. Wilderspin found himself reflected upon more to his disadvantage than otherwise. He had observed generally that it was the tendency of genius " not to care;"—to think so well of itself, or so absolutely to forget itself altogether, that it did not scruple to walk through the streets with a short pipe in its mouth, to go unshaven, and even publicly to exhibit itself in a state of physical and mental prostration. He saw that Genius could only carry out this sort of thing to an extent in proportion to its strength, and that even then the admiration which it attracted was strongly alloyed with pity and contempt. In fact Mr. Wilderspin perceived that to contemn society and its laws was in every way a grand mistake.

Accordingly he put down his helm, and went upon another tack. His first step was to remove to a more fashionable part of the town, and take Chambers in one of the Inns of Court. He now began to appear occasionally at the opera and in the stalls of theatres, and to take horse exercise in Rotten Row. He had not

moved long in this sphere before he made the acquaintance of several young gentlemen of fashion—a barrister
or two, several captains, a baronet, and the critic of an
influential morning journal. This gentleman was a very
different sort of person from the literary men whom
Mr. Wilderspin had been accustomed to meet. He
dressed in the height of the fashion, wore jewellery and
embroidered shirt-fronts, drank expensive drinks, dined

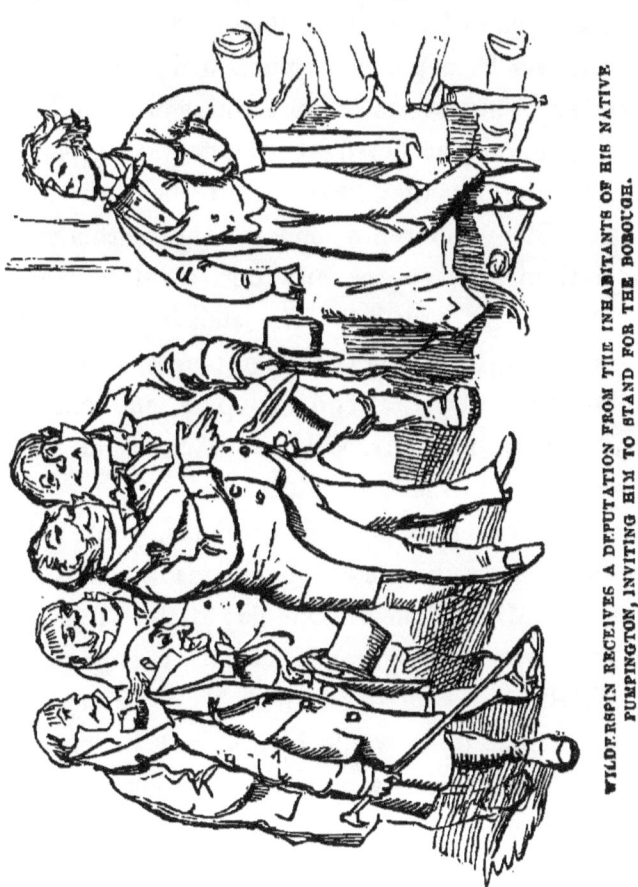

WILDERSPIN RECEIVES A DEPUTATION FROM THE INHABITANTS OF HIS NATIVE PUMPINGTON, INVITING HIM TO STAND FOR THE BOROUGH.

at select hotels, and never appeared at a theatre except
in full evening costume. He was so much in request in
society, that he always kept a pair of white gloves and an
opera-glass about his person. He spent nearly half his
time with white kid gloves on his hands, and an opera-
glass at his eyes. He was not a genius by any means, but
he had written a great deal, and his name was always mentioned among the celebrities of literature and art. He had
produced some of the worst plays and the worst books
that had ever been played or published ; but he was still
in request by managers and publishers, who could not resist the generally accepted fact that he was a great literary
celebrity, though they knew him to be a shallow pre-
tender. Mr. Wilderspin soon saw that in this society it
was extremely easy for any one to shine who could
simply play the "swell." The standard of excellence
here was to have high acquaintances, dress in the
fashion, drink claret, attend the opera, and smoke four-
penny cigars, and Mr. Wilderspin could do all these
things as well as the best of them.

Amongst other distinguished persons, whose acquaintance he made in this new sphere, was a parliamentary
agent, one Mr. Witcher. One day at the Club—a West
End one, where the entrance fee was twenty pounds—
Mr. Witcher, in a *téte-à-téte* with Mr. Wilderspin, asked
that gentleman if he would like a seat in Parliament.
This question, seriously propounded, took Mr. Wilderspin as much aback as if he had been asked if he would
like to be prime minister. He had indulged many fond
dreams, but the idea of sitting in the Legislature was a

thought that had never occurred to him. However, on recovering from his surprise, he made reply — that though his aspirations had never carried him to so high a point, he would feel proud of the position ; whereupon Mr. Witcher informed him, in a confidential whisper, that if he was prepared to spend a thousand pounds, he, Mr. Witcher, would guarantee his return for a borough in the West of England. The end of the matter was, that Mr. Wilderspin agreed to furnish the amount required, Mr. Witcher undertaking that at the end of the week a deputation of the electors should wait upon him, and formally request him to come forward as a candidate for the borough. At the appointed time a deputation of five gentlemen did wait upon Mr. Wilderspin at his Chambers ; and in a neat and graceful speech, Mr. W. thanked them for the honour they wished to confer upon him, and expressed his intention of going down to Pumpington—that was the name of the borough—and personally canvassing the electors.

In the mean time, Mr. Witcher favoured Mr. Wilderspin with much valuable advice as to the course of procedure in election matters. He dwelt with great emphasis on the various advantages of being an M.P., the patronage it conferred upon a person, the social influence it gave him, and, above all, the opportunities it afforded him of doing service to the country at large.

"Now, as to your politics, Mr. Wilderspin," said Mr. Witcher ; "you are liberal to the back bone I believe?"

Mr. Wilderspin *was* liberal to the backbone.

" You are, of course, in favour of Reform, and all that sort of thing ?"

Mr. Wilderspin declared Reform to be the watchword of his principles.

" Very good," said Mr. Witcher ; " go in for Reform, and promise everything they ask you ; and, with a thousand pounds at your back, you are sure to win."

Under Mr. Witcher's guidance, Mr. Wilderspin prepared an Address to the electors of Pumpington, which was duly published in the *Pumpington Gazette.* The Address was so thoroughly to the taste of the electors of the ancient borough, that on Mr. Wilderspin's arrival at the Pumpington railway station, he was drawn through the town in triumph.

For the second time in his life, Mr. Wilderspin had the gratification of seeing his name figuring in large print. Every dead wall and hoarding in Pumpington was pasted over with huge bills, calling upon the electors to " Vote for Wilderspin, the friend of Civil and Religious Liberty !" So enthusiastic were the non-electors in his favour, that they collected round his hotel, and cheered so vociferously and continuously, that Mr. Wilderspin was obliged to go out on the balcony and address them. He understood they were chiefly non-electors ; well, if he were returned to represent their borough in Parliament, he should take care that they should not be non-electors long. (Cheers.) Every man, woman, and child—he would not say woman and child—but every man there should have a vote. (Pro-

MR. WILDERSPIN IS DRAWN THROUGH HIS NATIVE TOWN IN TRIUMPH.

MR. WILDERSPIN ADDRESSES HIS CONSTITUENTS.

longed cheering, and cries of "Wilderspin for ever!"
Having thus stated his views to them, he hoped that they
would rally round him, and use the only influence which
as non-electors they possessed, to secure his triumphant
return for the borough of Pumpington. This, Mr.
Wilderspin's first public speech, was a decided success.
Though he did not say much, he got through what little
he did say so well, that his only wonder was that he
had never before discovered his aptitude for public life.
Mr. Wilderspin now devoted himself to a personal
canvass of the electors. In these expeditions he was
accompanied by Mr. Witcher and a local attorney of
the name of Twiggs, who undertook the task of personally introducing Mr. Wilderspin to the constituency
Messrs. Witcher and Twiggs carried a good deal of
money about with them, and frequently held private
conferences with the wives of ten-pound householders,
behind doors or in private rooms. Mr. Twiggs seemed
to be deeply interested in the various specimens of the
ceramic art which he saw, particularly when these specimens took the form of tea-pots. Mr. Witcher, for his
part, exhibited the greatest generosity wherever he went
—buying articles of poor shopkeepers, and forgetting
to take up the change; undertaking to pay off arrears
at loan offices; settling scores at taverns, and otherwise
spreading joy and happiness wherever he went. Meanwhile, Mr. Wilderspin addressed himself to the task of
admiring and playing with the electors' children. It
was astonishing what charming children he found in

ten-pound households. Perfect little angels they were, though their state of dirt was something incredible. But that did not prevent Mr. Wilderspin from taking them on his knee, treating them to bon-bons, and even kissing them when their noses were anything like approachable. In the course of the canvass Mr. Wilderspin made himself a great favourite with wives and mothers, and he flattered himself that favour in that quarter was generally a safe investment. The men were always more difficult to deal with, being generally less accessible to the force of hints. When a woman discovered Mr. Witcher handling her brown earthenware tea-pot, she would studiously look another way while he admired its beauties. But in these cases the only idea that her husband had in respect to the matter was that Mr. Witcher was going to pocket the article. The most difficult electors with whom Mr. Wilderspin had to deal were the publicans. Their votes and support depended in a very great measure indeed upon the handling of their pots. Their sagacity, however, in all instances was wonderful. In an interview of five minutes duration in the bar parlour, Mr. Wilderspin was able to convince the most stubborn of that stiff-necked generation that the proper party to vote for and support was the liberal candidate, viz. himself.

Much as the electors of Pumpington admired Mr. Wilderspin, it was not their desire that he should walk over the course, or even gain an easy victory. The town loved a little excitement, and did not often get it

MR. WILDERSPIN ENDEAVOURS TO INGRATIATE HIMSELF WITH THE CONSTI-
TUENCY, IN THE APPROVED FASHION.

MR. WILDERSPIN MAKES A LITTLE ARRANGEMENT WITH A TAVERN KEEPER—
A CASE OF THE PUBLICAN AND THE SINNER.

MR. WILDERSPIN IS ASSAILED BY THE SUPPORTERS OF THE BLOATED ARISTOCRAT,
THE CANDIDATE IN OPPOSITION,

BUT EVENTUALLY OBTAINS A SHOW OF (RATHER DIRTY) HANDS,

except at election time, and the electors of Pumpington, though, like Mr. Wilderspin himself, liberal to the back bone, liked to see a Tory candidate in the field, just to give a constitutional air to the proceedings. Thus it happened that Mr. Wilderspin met with a little of the rough as well as the smooth. His opponent, Lord Tom Noddy, was supported chiefly by the agriculturists, who, not being good at argument, assailed their opponents' principles by treating Mr. Wilderspin to a volley of vegetables and dead cats, which of course gave Mr. Wilderspin an opportunity of denouncing the conduct of the supporters of the " bloated aristocrat," the candidate in opposition. Mr. Wilderspin until this occasion had no idea of the power of the word " bloated" as applied to an aristocrat. He had spoken of his opponent simply as an aristocrat without producing any marked effect, but when, acting upon the hint of Mr. Witcher, he called him a " bloated aristocrat," the applause which he excited was perfectly deafening. " I say again," said Mr. Wilderspin, " bloated aristocrat." (Cries of " Bravo Wilderspin!" " No bloated aristocrats!" " Down with Lord Tom Noddy!" "Vote for Wilderspin!") To a reforming constituency, Mr. Wilderspin's principles could not but be in the highest degree satisfactory. He declared his intention of abolishing everything which seemed to be unpopular among the electors, and, on the same principle, he promised his support to all measures that seemed to be popular. With Mr. Twiggs at his back as prompter, he had no difficulty in answering the questions put to him, except when the mob made a noise and drowned Mr. Twiggs' whispers. He only made one mistake. "How about church-rates?" an Elector inquired. Mr. Wilderspin had imbibed conservative notions with respect to the church, in consequence of his father having been for many years associated in a humble capacity with a vestry, and was beginning a speech about "that venerable institution of the State, endeared to them all by——" when Mr. Twiggs pulled him by the coat tails, and whispered, "Abolish church rates;" whereupon Mr. Wilderspin continued, "that venerable institution of the State, which must be supported"— (Cries of "Not by church rates!")—"No, not by church rates," Mr. Wilderspin continued. "Well, well," cried the Elector who had asked the question, "what do you mean to do about them? Will you abolish them?" "Most certainly I will," said Mr. Wilderspin. This settled the matter: the show of hands was for Mr. Wilderspin.

ADVENTURE THE SIXTEENTH.

Mr. Wilderspin, having thanked his constituents, and perorated " in the language of that great poet, Cæsar Borgia,"—veni, vidi, vici, returns in triumph to London.—Mr. Wilderspin forswears the Stuarts, the Pope, and the devil; and vows to be loyal to the House of Guelph, Magna Charta, the British Constitution, in fact, Mr. Wilderspin takes all the oaths.—Mr. Wilderspin receives the congratulations of a Right Honourable Gentleman, a member of the government.—And of a noble lord, a member of the opposition.—And of a little shabby old man, whom he suspects to be a ticket porter "out of place."—And of a by no means " poor man from Manchester," with a great deal of work to do.—On returning home, Mr. Wilderspin finds Mary Jane laying a number of bills (private, for election expenses) on the table.—On the first reading, Mr. Wilderspin is in doubt whether he will be able to support them.

AFTER a severe contest, Mr. Wilderspin was elected Member of Parliament for the borough of Pumpington. His opponent, Lord Tom Noddy, had run him very close, and his majority, it must be confessed, was only One! What might have been the result had not a strong body of the non-electors insisted upon stopping and violently shaking hands with an old gentleman who was hurrying to the poll at the last moment, and who was too late to vote in consequence, was a question much discussed at the time, without any satisfactory solution of the point being arrived at, by reason of the old gentleman's inability—through serious injuries received—to say on which

MR. WILDERSPIN, HAVING THANKED HIS CONSTITUENTS, AND PEROBATED, "IN THE LANGUAGE OF THAT GREAT POET, CÆSAR BORGIA," "VINI, VEDI, VICI," RETURNS IN TRIUMPH TO LONDON.

side he intended to vote. The mystery was destined to
be solved afterwards, but mean time Mr. Wilderspin was
M.P. for Pumpington. In thanking the electors at the
close of the poll, Mr. Wilderspin declared that that moment was the happiest of his life. And Mr. Wilderspin
spoke the truth ; he had never been in such a whirl of
excitement before. Having embraced Messrs. Witcher
and Twiggs, and shaken hands with his committee, his
thoughts reverted to his aged parents. What delight
would be theirs when they heard that their son had
become a Member of Parliament! He was happy to
think that he could now do something for them. The
Customs occurred to him as being just the sort of haven
or th declining days of his venerable father ; Somer-
set House, or the War Office, the opening through which
his younger brother would step out into the high road of
a brilliant career. These dutiful considerations were Mr.
Wilderspin's first thought ;—and are they not the first
thought of every man who suddenly finds himself in a
position to assist his fellow-men? We are accustomed
to exhibit much virtuous indignation when a Cabinet
Minister confers appointments upon his own relatives or
friends ; but what is our own practice? You, sir, who
cry out so loudly against the Minister, what do you do
when you are appointed managing director of the Great
Direct South Railway? Do you give away your clerk-
ships to strangers? or do you confer them upon your
sons and nephews, or the sons and nephews of your in-
timate friends? Will you not give the preference to one

of your own, even if he be less capable than the stranger recommended to you? Will you not then, let a Cabinet Minister do as you do? Do you expect a Right Honourable to be less human than other folks? This is the question, above all others, about which there should be as little stone-throwing as possible.

Mr. Wilderspin took his departure from Pumpington in a barouche and pair, amid a demonstration of popular favour of the most flattering description. The non-electors followed him through the town in a vast mass, saluting him with cheers and cries of "Wilderspin for ever!" This class of the inhabitants had even more reason than those who enjoyed the franchise to be satisfied with their new Member; for during the election the partisans of Wilderspin, even though they had no vote, were treated with a courtesy which it would not have been prudent to offer to the voters. Ostensibly, the only acknowledgment to voters was thanks; but for the non-electors, there was bread-and-cheese and beer in unlimited quantities. Here, at least, the unenfranchised had the advantage over the possessors of a vote; and there were not a few of them who would have been sorry to see any Reform Bill passed which would have given them a vote and deprived them of their bread-and-cheese and beer. When Mr Wilderspin arrived at his Club in London he found about a score of letters awaiting him, all addressed, "Horatio Wilderspin, Esq., M.P" The epistles were nearly all from persons he had never heard of before. Three of them were from the secretaries of

projected insurance companies, asking him to become a
director. Others solicited his patronage and contribution
to hospitals and benevolent institutions. Some of the
writers confided to him their public wrongs, in the hope
that he would lay their cases before Parliament. Among
the heap there were several begging letters, and the
offer of a share in an old-established newspaper, which,
for a small annual subsidy, was ready to become Mr.
Wilderspin's organ. Some of these letters had been
written on the very day of his election—a fact which
was not a little gratifying to Mr. Wilderspin, since it

MR. WILDERSPIN FORSWEARS THE STUARTS, THE POPE, AND THE DEVIL, AND
VOWS TO BE LOYAL TO THE HOUSE OF GUELPH, MAGNA CHARTA, THE BRITISH
CONSTITUTION—IN FACT, MR. WILDERSPIN TAKES ALL THE OATHS.

showed that a portion of the public had been interested
in his success.

In due course Mr. Wilderspin took the oaths and
his seat, being introduced on the occasion by an honourable gentleman who volunteered his services in the
hope of securing Mr. Wilderspin as a supporter of his
annual motion. Mr. Wilderspin had been afraid that
he might be slighted by the great personages in the
House. He was aware that a majority of the members
were aristocrats, or connexions of aristocratic families,

MR. WILDERSPIN RECEIVES THE CONGRATU-   AND OF A NOBLE LORD, A MEMBER OF THE
LATIONS OF A RIGHT HONOURABLE GEN-   OPPOSITION.
TLEMAN, A MEMBER OF THE GOVERN-
MENT.

and he was apprehensive that he, who had sprung from the humbler classes of society, might be tabooed by them. But he was soon relieved from his uneasy feeling on this head. An important debate was going on, upon the result of which hung the fate of the Ministry. Both sides were eagerly and anxiously hunting up supporters. Mr. Wilderspin had no sooner taken his seat than a Right Honourable Baronet came across the floor and shook hands with him, congratulating him on his success at Pumpington, and trusting that his (the Right Honourable Baronet's) party would receive his support. This Right Honourable gentleman was one of the "Whips" of the Government. The leading "Whip" of the Opposition no sooner saw his rival in possession of the new Member than he hastened to dispute for the prize. This gentleman also shook hands with him in the most cordial manner. Mr. Wilderspin felt in some danger of being torn in pieces between them. One pulled him one way, the other another, each desirous of a chat with him in private. Both succeeded eventually ; but Mr. Wilderspin was so confused by the volley of compliments, private communications, and political hints which were poured upon him, that he was unable to say which was the Tory and which the Whig. When the two Whips introduced him to the chiefs of their respective parties he was as much in a fog as ever, for though he had often heard of the Noble Lords and Right Honourable Gentlemen, he had never seen any of them before, and the popular portraits were no guide to their recognition. For example, when he was introduced to the Chancellor of the Exchequer, instead of finding him, as he had been led to imagine him, a youthful-looking person with long cork-screw ringlets, a splendid waiscoat, and a profusion of jewellery, he beheld a plainly-dressed personage, considerably advanced in age, stooping very much, without a trace of ringlets, or even so much as a ring on his finger. A celebrated Noble Lord, whom he had expected to present an aspect of great severity, he found to be a jaunty, good-humoured old gentleman with no particular appearance about him beyond that of being unsteady on his legs, rather deaf, and slightly blind. This Noble Lord, however, was exceedingly condescending and polite, and on parting with Mr. Wilderspin, hoped he would have the pleasure of seeing that gentleman at her Ladyship's soirée on the following Saturday.

Another celebrated Noble Lord to whom Mr. Wilderspin was introduced was a great disappointment to him in point of personal appearance. He was a very little old man, very thin and very shabby-looking. His hat—a shocking bad one—was too big for him, and came down half over his face. His coat had probably been made in the year that he carried his Reform Bill, and it was as much worn out as his Bill. A popular Member, who was then becoming a great power in the House, presented in personal appearance a marked contrast to the two Noble Lords ; yet he did not come up to Mr. Wilderspin's *beau ideal* of a great statesman. He was sturdy and vigorous, it is true, but his prevailing aspect was that of a retired prize-fighter. Peaceful in his policy, he was in the highest degree pugnacious both in speech and action. Mr. Wilderspin was rather overawed by this personage, until he invited him to smoke a cigar with him on the Terrace facing the river, when he soon found out that this terrible demagogue was a remarkably jolly fellow. But what surprised him most was that several young sprigs of nobility of the Tory party came and sought this demagogue's company,

AND OF A LITTLE SHABBY OLD MAN, WHOM HE SUSPECTS TO BE A TICKET PORTER "OUT OF PLACE." AND OF A BY NO MEANS "POOR MAN FROM MANCHESTER," WITH A GREAT DEAL OF WORK TO DO.

and walked up and down with him, discussing politics
in the most amicable manner.   It was wonderful how
nearly those Noble Lords agreed with the Demagogue
down on the Terrace, and how widely they differed from
him upstairs in the House.   "What a pity it is,"
thought Mr. Wilderspin, "that the affairs of the nation
are not discussed down on this esplanade, with iced
sherry and regalias."

Mr. Wilderspin's first day's experience of Parliament
made him sensible of a fact which he had not recog-

ON RETURNING HOME, MR. WILDERSPIN FINDS MARY JANE LAYING A NUMBER OF
BILLS (PRIVATE, FOR ELECTION EXPENSES,) ON THE TABLE.   ON THE FIRST
READING, MR. WILDERSPIN IS IN DOUBT, WHETHER HE WILL BE ABLE TO SUP-
PORT THEM.

nised before, viz., that it was the vote and not the man that was respected there. He was fully aware that the attention that had been paid to him by illustrious statesmen was not prompted by any regard for Horatio Wilderspin, as an individual and a member of society, but as a Member of Parliament and a voter on divisions. Still, Mr. Wilderspin felt that he had been highly honoured, and justly so, for is not a man's power essentially a part of himself?

It generally happens in life, that when your spirits are at the highest pitch there is something at hand to dash them. What a pity it is that the case does not admit of a *vice versâ!* On Mr. Wilderspin's return from the House he found his table groaning under the weight of election bills. Mr. Witcher had not kept faith with him. He had paid a thousand pounds on the understanding that that amount would cover all expenses ; but here were bills to the amount of at least a thousand more.

ADVENTURE THE SEVENTEENTH.

Mr Wilderspin, M.P., having examined his election accounts, is troubled in his mind.—Mr. Wilderspin, M.P., receives a ticket from the Lord Chamberlain to attend a Levée.—The "Honorable Gentleman" consults his noble friend "The Baron" as to his costume.—Mr. Wilderspin, M.P., in the character of courtier;—Astonishes the weak minds of his neighbours, and gives rise to the report that "there is a masquerade at the Holborn to-night."—Mr. Wilderspin, M.P., arrives at the Palace and presents his credentials.—Mr. Wilderspin, M.P., has the honour of being presented to his Sovereign.

THE whirl of excitement in which Mr. Wilderspin had recently passed his life had left him but little time for philosophical reflection. When at last he obtained a quiet moment he found that his accounts—both those of his mental and monetary estate—were greatly in need of being posted up. After a good think, aided by the stimulus of a pipe of tobacco, he began to suspect that a public life did not tend to conserve the conscience and the moral perceptions in a condition altogether healthy. He felt that he was not so strong in the *mens conscius recti* as he had been when he moved in a humbler sphere. He found that in his public capacity he had been doing things which the private man could not approve. It flashed upon him reproachfully that he had humbugged his constituents; that he had wil-

MR. WILDERSPIN M.P., HAVING EXAMINED HIS ELECTION AC-
COUNTS IS TROUBLED IN HIS MIND.

MR. WILDERSPIN M.P., RECEIVES A TICKET FROM THE LORD
CHAMBERLAIN, "TO ATTEND A LEVÉE."

fully closed his eyes to practices which were positively dishonest; and that he had allowed himself to be cajoled and flattered. Altogether, he had not so good an opinion of himself as he had had when he was in a humbler position. Then his pecuniary affairs gave him some uneasiness. He had paid a thousand pounds for his seat in Parliament, and claims for another thousand had still to be discharged. On examining his banker's book, he found that he had only £2,000 in available cash left, having spent £2,000 in personal expenses, and invested the remainder in a Welsh coal-mine, whose prospects were reported to be anything but brilliant. There is no doubt, that, if his quiet moments had been prolonged, Mr. Wilderspin would have taken steps to put himself straight both mentally and monetarily. But he who enters upon public life throws himself into a rapid which carries him ever onward, leaving him neither time nor opportunity to shape his course. Glory, after all, is but another species of intoxicating drink. When you have imbibed a certain quantity, you lose the power of resisting its influence. In what respect is an ambitious man better then a drunkard, if his ambition be not a worthy one? Another glass; another advantage gained—sensation at the bottom of it all. Indeed, it may he argued that the drunkard, who is so much despised, is a better man than he who indulges a craving for wealth, for power, or for influence. The drunkard hurts no one but himself. Can the same be said of the money-grubber, who grinds down his fellow-men, or

the tyrant who enslaves a State that he may be King?
O! much slandered drink! shall I, who daily give
thanks for thy invigorating influence, be guilty of the
cant which represents thee as the worst of all evils?
Thou hast rarely been my master, O Drink! but when,
on high days and holidays, thou hast asserted thy sway,
and laid me at thy feet, I have awoke from my bondage
with less sense of shame than when I have entertained
a malignant thought, or refused a friend a service which
I had it in my power to render him. I speak not of
speechlessness ; but *quem non fecundi calices fecere
disertum et felicem?* It would have been better for
Mr. Wilderspin had he taken to draughts of brandy,
instead of draughts of glory. An overdose of the
former brings its corrective in the shape of a next
morning's headache; but there is no soda-water for the
intoxication of glory. It grows upon what it feeds.

Mr. Wilderspin was on the point of resolving to turn
over a new leaf, when his good intentions were demolished at one blow, by the receipt of a ticket admitting
him to Her Majesty's Levée. This was, in fact, an invitation from his Sovereign! Come Diogenes, bring
your lantern—fill your lamp with oil, and well trim the
wick; and let us look for the man who possesses the
strength of mind to resist putting himself in silk tights,
and buckling on a sword, to walk in, crab fashion,
before his Sovereign. Here is a stoic, a scoffer at all
things sublime : why, he is already dressed a couple
of hours before-hand ! There you see a Chartist orator

—one who denounces Kings and Queens, and talks of the Sovereignty of the People—behold with what satisfaction he is arraying himself—mark the flush of excitement on his face! Yonder is a *savan*, a grave and reverend signior, practising walking backwards before his glass!

Now, Mr. Wilderspin was neither a cynic nor a Chartist, nor was he a *savan;* and, consequently, it was not at all surprising that on receiving the Lord Chamberlain's ticket, he should have at once rushed off to procure a court dress. In his innocence of the fact that the great majority of people who go to Court hire their dresses for the day from theatrical costumiers and Jew clothes men, Mr. Wilderspin was on the point of calling on a Court tailor and ordering an entirely new suit, when a Club friend informed him of the general and more economical practice. Mr. Wilderspin was not pleased to think that the *habitues* of the Court were in the habit of presenting themselves before Her Majesty in borrowed, second-hand suits; but, on considering the difference of expense between the borrowed suit and the new one, he decided to take his friend's advice. Accordingly he applied to a gentleman of the Hebrew persuasion, popularly believed to be a Baron, and was soon accommodated with all the articles requisite for a Court toilette. When he had arrayed himself—not without considerable difficulty—in the Baron's garments and came to look at himself in the glass, he was of opinion that the costume was decidedly becoming. The

THE "HONOURABLE GENTLEMAN" CONSULTS HIS NOBLE FRIEND "THE BARON" AS TO HIS COSTUME.

MR. WILDERSPIN, M.P. IN THE CHARACTER OF COURTIER;

only drawback to his feeling perfectly at his ease was the sword, which was apt to get between his legs when he walked about, threatening occasionally to trip him up.

Mr. Wilderspin dressed several hours before the time, in order to rehearse the " business" of the scene in which he was about to act. To his great joy, he found that his old friend and guide, the *Hints on Etiquette*, contained full instructions as to Court behaviour. It was laid down in that admirable work, that the " party," on entering the presence of his Sovereign, should ap-

ASTONISHES THE WEAK MINDS OF HIS NEIGHBOURS, AND GIVES RISE TO THE RE-
PORT " THERE IS A MASQUERADE AT THE HOLBORN TO NIGHT."

proach the Throne with a series of graceful inclinations of the head; that, on arriving opposite his Sovereign, he should make a profound bow, and pause for a moment, in case Her Majesty should offer him her hand to kiss.   In the event of such graciousness being extended to him, he was to fall gracefully upon one knee, gently take Her Majesty's gloved hand, and respectfully put the tips of her fingers to his lips.   It was not, however, etiquette to smack the lips in performing this ceremony On leaving the Sovereign's presence the "party" was instructed to keep his face to the Throne, and retire backwards, bowing gracefully until he had left the apartment.   Putting a pillow up in his arm-chair to represent his Sovereign, Mr. Wilderspin practised the above evolutions for fully an hour, and was at last enabled to acquit himself to his entire satisfaction.

There was no small sensation in the street when he stepped across the pavement in full Court costume to enter his cab.   I have shown in a former chapter that there are occasions when departure from one's own door in a cab is a painful trial.   There are other times, however, when it becomes a matter of pride.   For instance, when you are stepping into the vehicle with your lovely and accomplished bride; when you are full dressed for the Opera; or, as in Mr. Wilderspin's case, when you are arrayed for a Levée.   Mr. W. was not a little proud to show himself in a laced coat, with a sword at his side; and in passing to his carriage paused for a moment to put on his gloves, that he might give the neighbours an opportunity of seeing him. The street boys, who, with that strong instinct for sights which so eminently characterises them, had collected in a crowd round the door steps, were deeply interested in Mr. Wilderspin's make-up Whatever the neighbours, who watched the proceedings from the windows opposite, might have thought on the subject, the opinion of the boys was that the gentleman was going to a Masquerade at "the Holborn," and wanted to be there in good time. When the cab started, they expressed their approval of the proceeding by keeping pace with the vehicle, and cheering its distinguished inmate to the end of the street.

Having arrived at the Palace, and presented his credentials at the outer door, Mr. Wilderspin was passed on, from one official to another, until he found himself in an ante-room crowded to excess by a throng of gentlemen arrayed like himself. Every individual there assembled suffered the greatest inconvenience, and even pain, from the fact that every other individual had a sword sticking out behind, which was continually being poked into his stomach or the small of his back. The conversation was thus entirely and wholly of an apologetic nature, for whenever any one moved or turned round, some other person near him received a poke in the ribs. This person in his turn started back and gave some one else a poke, to be passed on *ad infinitum.* It was a strange, motley, ill-smelling assembly. There were members of Parliament, barristers, officers, Lord

MR. WILDERSPIN, M.P. ARRIVES AT THE PALACE AND PRESENTS HIS CREDENTIALS.

Lieutenants, Doctors of Law, Physic, and Divinity, young parsons, architects, builders, Lord Mayors, Aldermen, Sheriffs, ambassadors, envoys, attachés, poets, artists, and even a few newspaper reporters. When Mr. Wilderspin saw one of those last-mentioned gentlemen, a person whom he had last seen at the "Blue Lamb," thickly haranguing the bar at two o'clock in the morning, he began to think that to be presented at Court was not such a choice privilege after all. He was very much shocked indeed when this gentleman slapped him

on the shoulder and said, loud enough for the Lord
Mayor and the Poet Laureate to hear :

"Holloa, my boy ; ain't this dry work ? Don't you
wish you were within reach of a pint of porter ?"

"Hush !" said Mr. Wilderspin ; "remember where
you are."

"Oh, I see ; you haven't been here before," said Mr.
Bang, the stenographer ; " I make a point of attending
every Levée ; have done it for years ; fine thing to have
your name in the *Court Circular.* I wonder more fellows don't do it."

Mr. Wilderspin ventured to say that he had always
imagined it was a very difficult thing to get an introduction to Court.

"Nothing of the sort, my dear fellow," said Mr.
Bang ; "nothing more easy. Ask any member of
Parliament, or any one who has been presented, to put
your name down, and the thing's done. The Lord
Chamberlain don't know you from Adam ; and if he
did, he dare not refuse you a ticket, if there's nothing
against your character. Why look at that fat man over
yonder : he's a sweating tailor, and makes his Royal
Highness's breeches, by the way. He's about the only
man here who hasn't got a hired dress on ; makes it
himself, you know. Don't you smell the old clo' ?
Do you know, I have got an uncomfortable sensation
about the back of my neck. Take my advice ; when
you get home, send your suit back to the Baron as soon
as possible, and take a bath."

Mr. Wilderspin was not sorry when his name was called out by the Chamberlain and he was enabled to get away from Mr. Bang, whose conversation was getting highly unpleasant.

At the door of the State Apartment Mr. Wilderspin was met by the Right Honourable gentleman who had undertaken to introduce him, and was at once conducted into the royal presence. His name being again called out, he followed his guide across the floor, bending gracefully at every step until he arrived in front of the Throne, when he made a profound obeisance—but so suddenly that the point of his sword tipped up and struck his Right Honourable friend on the nose. Her Majesty, in some alarm, held out her hand, as if to prevent further accident, and Mr. Wilderspin, taking this for the signal to kiss her hand, was advancing to avail himself of that high privilege, when his introducer pulled him back by the skirts of the coat. The effect of this abrupt act was, that Mr. Wilderspin's sword got between his legs and very nearly upset him. His equanimity was so overturned by this *contre-temp*, that his attempt to walk backwards from Her Majesty's presence ended in his treading on the toes of a gouty old courtier, and making him bellow out in a most irregular and unseemly manner, greatly to the amusement of Her Majesty, who was obliged to smother her laughter in her pocket-handkerchief.

Overwhelmed with chagrin and confusion, Mr. Wilderspin would have been glad to escape at once from observation, and hide his diminished head in seclusion ; but, unfortunately, the process of getting out of the Palace was as difficult and dangerous as the process of getting in. Once more he had to encounter an array of sword points, in a crowded ante-room, where those who followed him from Her Majesty's presence caused much merriment by relating his misadventures in the Throne Room. For fully half an hour he had the mortification of being hustled about and poked with swords, while the courtiers on all sides of him were indulging in roars of laughter at his expense.

Mr. Wilderspin was not in the habit of making rash vows ; but when he got outside, he was heard to invoke a dire calamity on his head if anybody ever caught him at a Levée again.

MR. WILDERSPIN, M.P. HAS THE HONOUR OF BEING PRESENTED TO HIS SOVEREIGN.

ADVENTURE THE EIGHTEENTH.

Mr. Wilderspin is waited upon by a deputation of gentlemen (and
scholars) personally interested in the repeal of the Taxes on
Knowledge, and informs them that he has no doubt of being
able to induce the ministers to listen to their appeal.—Mr.
Wilderspin goes down to the House, and finds a number of his
constituents waiting to consult him as to the "Pumpington no
Taxes Bill," which he has undertaken to introduce.—The noble
lord at the head of Her Majesty's government being pressed by
his honourable friend Mr. Wilderspin, on the subject of the
Taxes on Knowledge, replies as above.—The hopes held out
by Mr. Wilderspin's right honourable friend, the First Lord of
the Admiralty.—Those of his right honourable friend, the
Chancellor of the Exchequer.—Mr. Wilderspin addresses himself to the interests of the nation at large, and makes a great speech
on Reform.

MR. WILDERSPIN had little dreamt how uneasily lay the
head of a Member of Parliament. He had scarcely enjoyed the dignity for a week before he was inundated by
hundreds of letters, petitions, and memorials, and his door
besieged by scores of applicants for interviews at all
times of the day, and even night. All the new public
companies in the metropolis (and some of the old ones
to boot) seemed to want him for a director. Every
movement, political, social, literary or artistic, sought his
name and support. Everybody whom he had ever

known wanted his interest with some Minister or head of a department, to obtain a place, either for himself, or his son, or his nephew, or the son or the nephew of some one else. He was besought to become a member of the Society for the Promotion of Vote By Pitch and Toss ; of the Society for Legalizing Marriage with a Deceased Wife's Aunt ; of the Society for Opposing Marriage with a Deceased Wife's Aunt ; of the societies for the suppression of crime, intoxicating liquors, churchrates, toll-bars, statute fairs, the Corporation of the City of London, barrel-organs, taxes, and the Book of Common Prayer. There was, in fact, nothing under the sun which he was not asked to aid in suppressing nor any thing which he was not asked to foster and support. The reading of scores of memorials, and listening to endless speeches, on every variety of topic, entangled his ideas to such an extent that he was quite unable to distinguish between one thing and another. The Deceased Wife's Aunt ran against toll-bars ; the Corporation of the City of London mixed itself up with intoxicating liquors ; and the Book of Common Prayer agglomerated itself with statute fairs, church-rates crime, and barrel organs.

Mr Wilderspin was in despair, and would fain have resigned his seat in favour of Lord Tom Noddy or any one else. On reflection, however, he felt that a great public duty devolved upon him, which he was bound to use every effort to discharge. Finding it utterly useless to attempt single-handed to answer all the letters and deputations which came to him, he engaged a secretary, and endeavoured to systematize the business. On the model of Alfred the Great, he divided his time into portions,—so many hours to reading, so many to writing, receiving deputations, &c., and so many to rest and devotion. The deputations would certainly have swallowed up an undue portion of his time, if he had not laid down a rule, that no deputation should remain more than ten minutes—a regulation which Mr. Wilderspin had seen carried out with great success at coffee-houses with regard to the newspaper, and at Mr. Richardson's booth with regard to the tragedy. One of the earliest interviews granted was to a deputation of gentlemen (and scholars) interested in the repeal of the paper-duty. The deputation consisted of the proprietors of cheap newspapers and periodicals, who were really earnest in the matter, and a few authors and leading article writers, who came merely for a lark. As some of these latter were personally known to Mr. Wilderspin, he was pleased to make an exception in the case as regards time, and begged that they would enter into the subject at length.

This the proprietors did not fail to do, laying great stress upon the fact, that the chief object sought was the benefit of authors. When Mr. Chicory said this, Mr. Wilderspin thought he detected Mr. Rasper, the slashing critic, significantly putting his tongue in his cheek. Another great object, said Mr. Chicory, was the education of the people. During many years, that gentleman said, he had been engaged in the production of books of an educational nature, but the effect of the paper duty had been to limit his sphere of action, and, consequently, to check the spread of education. Mr. Chicory having given elaborate statistics of the operation of the obnoxious duty, was followed by other proprietors in succession, who all declared that they had no other object at heart than the benefit of authors and the enlightenment of the people. Mr. Wilderspin was *highly* pleased with this disinterestedness, and, complimented the various proprietors on the zeal which they displayed in so good a cause. He would certainly give his best attention to the subject, and use every means in his power to bring about the repeal of the impost; and, finally he would say that the literary profession were very much indebted to Mr. Chicory and others, for the efforts they were making to forward their interests.

Mr. Rasper (Irish) here stood forward and begged to say a few words on behalf of the literary profession. He, himself, was a mimber of it; his constitutional modesty would not let him say a distinguished mimber —but still, a mimber of that honourable profession. He was quite sure that the publishers and proprietors, in seeking the repeal of the paper duty, were solely influenced by a philanthropic desire to put money in the pockets of the honourable profession to which he had the honour to belong, and to extend the benefits of education to the community at large ; but unther existing circumstances, they were not able to do so. They made great sacrifices for the honourable profession to

MR. WILDERSPIN IS WAITED UPON BY A DEPUTATION OF GENTLEMEN (AND SCHOLARS) PERSONALLY INTERESTED IN THE REPEAL OF THE TAXES ON KNOWLEDGE, AND INFORMS THEM THAT HE HAS NO DOUBT OF BEING ABLE TO INDUCE THE MINISTERS TO LISTEN TO THEIR APPEAL.

which he belonged. Notwithstanding the pressure of this tax upon them, they paid the mimbers of the profession to which he belonged from seven and sixpence to one pound one for a leading article. Now, under existing circumstances, that was a great price for them to pay, if it was not quite so high a price as mimbers of his profession could desire to receive. But see what would be the benefit to the mimbers of his profession if this obnoxious impost were removed. Why, the proprietors would be able to advance the price of a leading article by eighteen pence. Mimbers of his profession would then get from nine shillings to one pound two and sixpence for a leading article, which, it was needless for him to say, would enable mimbers of his profession to live like gentlemen and save money. Then, in the book trade the advantage would be equally great. His friend, Mr. Chicory, whose efforts on behalf of authors had received the commendation of noble lords and mimbers of Parliament, was in the habit of giving thirty shillings a sheet for the translation of French works on history, politics, and other subjects requiring great accuracy. He had no doubt that his friend made great sacrifices in giving so much : but what would be the case if the paper duty were repealed? Why, his friend would be able to give thirty-one and sixpence for such work. The British author would then be able to procure at least one meal a day, which, his friend (Mr. Chicory) would bear him out in saying, was all that he required. He thanked the publishers

and proprietors for their benevolent intentions towards
the mimbers of his profession ; and he believed that the
day was not far distant when the efforts they were
making would place authors and journalists in as good
a position as that now enjoyed by other trades, such as
bricklayers and plumbers and glaziers.

The deputation, having thanked Mr. Wilderspin for
the courteous attention he had accorded to them, then
retired.

Deputations lay in wait for Mr. Wilderspin at all
corners. If they could not find him at his house, they
went down and waited for him in Westminster Hall or
the Lobby. There is always a crowd of people waiting
for members at the House. It may be a question if any
member ever, on any single occasion, was allowed to pass
into the House without being stopped by some one so-
liciting to speak to him about something or other.
Orders for the gallery are as sedulously sought of M.P.s,
as orders for the boxes are sought of the managers of
theatres. Then there is always some constituent reminding the honourable gentleman of the support he
gave him at his election, and the obligation he is consequently under to get his (the elector's) son into the
Custom House, or some other hospital for the families
of M.P.s and their friends. There is also the constituent with a claim upon the Government, who, as he
never gets redress, never ceases from troubling, but
grows grey, haunting New Palace Yard and Westminster
Hall. Mr. Wilderspin endeavoured to do his best for

all; and whenever he spoke to a member of the Government on any subject, he invariably met with hopeful
courtesy, and a promise that the matter would have his
best attention.   These assurances were often accompanied by promises which, of course, were never fulfilled.

Mr. Wilderspin having watched the proceedings of
the House for some time, became ambitious of making
a speech.   He went down night after night ready

MR. WILDERSPIN GOES DOWN TO THE HOUSE, AND FINDS A NUMBER OF HIS CONSTI
TUENTS WAITING TO CONSULT HIM AS TO THE "PUMPINGTUN NO TAXES BILL,"
WHICH HE HAS UNDERTAKEN TO INTRODUCE.

THOSE OF HIS RIGHT HONOURABLE FRIEND, THE CHANCELLOR OF THE EXCHEQUER.

THE NOBLE LORD AT THE HEAD OF HER MAJESTY'S GOVERNMENT BEING PRESSED BY HIS HONOURABLE FRIEND, MR. WILDERSPIN, ON THE SUBJECT OF THE TAXES ON KNOWLEDGE, REPLIES AS ABOVE.

THE HOPES HELD OUT BY MR. WILDERSPIN'S RIGHT HONOURABLE FRIEND, THE FIRST LORD OF THE ADMIRALTY.

R

primed with an address on Reform, but for a long time
was unable to catch the Speaker's eye. Whenever he
got up, the Speaker persistently turned his face towards
some other Honourable, or Right Honourable gentleman,
who had risen at the same time, and it happened, pro-
vokingly, that some one always rose at the same time
that Mr. Wilderspin did. Mr. Wilderspin was at length
so indignant at the perversity of the Speaker's eye, that
he had thoughts of bringing in a Bill to regulate the
orbit of that optic. At length, one evening, when a
Right Honourable gentleman, on whom the Speaker had
fixed his eyes, delayed getting upon his legs until he
arranged his papers, Mr. Wilderspin started up suddenly,
and, in so doing, knocked down his hat. The noise
attracted the attention of the Speaker in the direction
of Mr. Wilderspin, and that gentleman was at last successful in catching the eye of the Chair. Having accomplished this much, and said '' Sir,'' he was of course
entitled to go on. But Mr. Wilderspin found it not so
easy to go on. Members on all hands were turning
round to look at him, and he became very nervous.
'' Sir,'' he repeated again and again, without being able
to get out another word. At length he went on, '' Unaccustomed as I am to public speaking,'' (a laugh);
'' unaccustomed as I am to public speaking, Sir,'' (renewed laughter), '' I nevertheless object to the terms in
which Mr. Merrypebble'' (cries of '' Order''), '' I repeat
in which Mr. Merrypebble'' (renewed cries of '' Order,
order.'') '' Sir, I am a young member of this House,

but I am still a member of this House, and as such, I am entitled to be heard ; and I again repeat that Mr. Merrypebble," (" Order, order," and laughter). " Will you then allow me to state that—I—ah—hold—ah—that I—ah—entirely agree on this important question with Mr. Bluff."—(Renewed cries of " Order, order," amid which the honourable gentleman sat down.)

Mr. Wilderspin resumed his seat burning with indignation. He had been denied a hearing—he had been hounded down in the British House of Commons. He would refer his case to the House of Lords—to the Queen herself—but first he would write to the *Times*. With this resolve he put on his hat, strode down the Floor of the House, and was making his way past the Speaker's chair, when he was assailed with cries of " Order," uttered in louder accents than before. Mr. Wilderspin darted through the little door behind the Speaker, as if the Serjeant at Arms had been pursuing him sword in hand, threw himself into a cab, and drove home in disgust, entirely innocent of the fact that it was against the etiquette of the House for a member to call another by his name or to pass the Speaker with his hat on.

MR. WILDESPIN ADDRESSES HIMSELF TO THE INTERESTS OF THE NATION AT LARGE, AND MAKES A GREAT SPEECH ON REFORM.

ADVENTURE THE NINETEENTH.

Mr. Wilderspin having been convicted of bribery, corruption, and treating at Pumpington, suddenly finds himself unseated. —Being beset by " bums," Mr. Wilderspin takes a desperate step, and leaves his " bums" behind him.—After many hair-breadth escapes over spiked walls, to the imminent danger of his peg-tops, Mr. Wilderspin finds himself in the clutch of the law.—And is caged in a sponging house.—Mr. Wilderspin at length understands what is a " Habeas Corpus."—Mr. Wilderspin takes up his residence with Her Majesty, in her palace of " the Bench."—Reception of Mr. Wilderspin on the Grand Parade.

MR. WILDERSPIN's parliamentary career was destined to be a very short one. His unsuccessful opponent, Lord Tom Noddy, presented a petition against his return, and the matter having been referred to a Committee, it was eventually declared that Horatio Wilderspin was "not duly elected for the Borough of Pumpington." The truth must be told—Mr. Wilderspin was clearly convicted of bribery, corruption, and treating, both by himself and his agents. The news of his defeat was a heavy blow to Mr. Wilderspin. He did not care so much for the loss of his seat, and the dignity attaching thereto; he could have borne with that, but to be branded with infamy before the whole country, that, to his feeling and sensitive nature, was a sharp thorn indeed. He was perfectly conscious that he had been guilty of the malpractices which had led to his being unseated ; but he could not conceive how he could ever have stooped to acts of such palpable dishonesty. He tried to recall the frame of mind in which he had set out with Messrs. Witcher and Twiggs to canvass the electors. He well remembered having purchased the support and partisanship of a publican ; but he could not call to mind that he felt any compunction of conscience in doing so. He had quietly turned his face another way when Messrs. Witcher and Twiggs converted damp tea-leaves in a brown earthenware tea-pot, into crisp, dry leaves of the great tree which flourishes in Threadneedle-street. He had put sovereigns into his coat pocket that he might pull them out with his pocket-handkerchief, and leave them on the floors of humble electors. He had overcome the political scruples of a hatter by purchasing a dozen furry, four-and-ninepenny *chapeaux* at a guinea each. He pretended to think children beautiful who were positively hideous. In fact he had bribed, treated, and lied, right and left ; and he had never blushed for himself until now. When Mr. Wilderspin devoted himself to reflection, his philosophy always hit the right nail on the head. He saw that he had been blinded by the glare of glory which was beginning to dawn upon him; that his moral perceptions had been blunted by his ambition ; that he had sunk the private man in the public man, and that, for want of time to pause and reflect, he had been hurried onward from one unworthy act to another. But, like most other wicked people, Mr. Wilderspin did not come to repentance until his wickedness proved a failure. Then he became very penitent, and resumed a long-intermitted practice of saying his prayers o' nights. How was it he couldn't say his prayers when he was canvassing at Pumpington? He remembered that it was when he went down to Pumpington that he left off his devotions. On turning the matter over in his mind, Mr. Wilderspin came to the conclusion that a member of Parliament was like the rich man of the parable, the difficulty of whose Heavenward progress was as that of a camel which might attempt to pass through the eye of a needle. Thus, although he had been hurled from his high dignity, and had incurred a public disgrace, he congratulated himself that he was once more in a position to exercise those wholesome private virtues which tend to sustain self-respect and an approving conscience.

But, alas! Mr. Wilderspin's calamity did not end here. The expenses of defending the petition of his opponent had exhausted his monetary resources, and left him deeply in debt. In the hope of realising his Welsh shares, he endeavoured to stave off legal proceedings by giving bills to his creditors. How easy it is to give a bill! What honest man who ever gave a bill did not feel, at the moment, that when the time came he would manage to take it up somehow or other?

MR. WILDERSPIN HAVING BEEN CONVICTED OF BRIBERY, CORRUPTION, AND TREATING, AT PUMPINGTON, SUDDENLY FINDS HIMSELF UNSEATED.

BEING BESET BY "BUMS," MR. WILDERSPIN TAKES A DESPERATE STEP, AND LEAVES HIS "BUMS" BEHIND HIM.

AFTER MANY HAIR-BREADTH ESCAPES OVER SPIKED WALLS, TO THE IMMINENT DANGER OF HIS PEG-TOPS, MR. WILDERSPIN FINDS HIMSELF IN THE CLUTCH OF THE LAW.

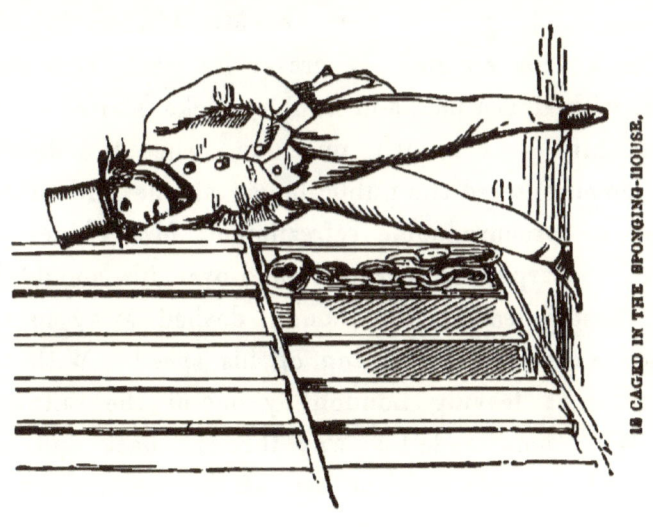

IS CAGED IN THE SPONGING-HOUSE.

Does not every man who gives a bill feel the same sort of relief as if he had paid the money? "Thank goodness," we say, "that man is paid." But how the days and weeks tumble over each other when you have bills to take up! If you have money to receive, three months seem an age; if you have money to pay, they seem a week. When Mr. Wilderspin gave his creditors bills, the weeks flew by like milestones on a railway journey. He was at the terminus of three months before he knew where he was. On receiving intimation of judgment, Mr. Wilderspin fled. He had been haunted for some time with visions of sheriffs' officers watching his door. He had seen a Jewish-looking person, in an alpaca hat, walking backwards and forwards on the other side of the way, and he felt satisfied he was watching to see that he (Mr. Wilderspin) did not make his escape. Wherever he went, smouchey men, with alpaca hats and knobby sticks, started up to alarm him. At length, one day, when the Jewish gentleman entered the public-house at the end of the street, to procure some refreshment, Mr. Wilderspin seized his carpet-bag, threw a plaid over his shoulders, and, hastily leaving the house, dashed away in the opposite direction at the top of his speed. With the intention of leaving London by one of the railways, Mr. Wilderspin made his way through back and unfrequented streets, until he had left the region of danger far behind him. His alarm had now subsided, and he was congratulating himself on being able to keep out of the way until he could sell his Welsh shares, when he felt a gentle tap on his shoulder. Turning sharply round, he encountered a darksome personage with a large hooked nose, who, in a facetious manner, expressed his pleasure at falling in with Mr. Wilderspin. "The fact is, Mr. Wilderspin," said he, "I have been looking for you. You will see by this," he continued, pulling out a piece of paper, "I am empowered by the Sheriff of Middlesex to—"

Mr. Wilderspin himself supplied the rest—"To arrest me!"

"Exactly so," said the gentleman with the hooked nose.

"Well," said Mr. Wilderspin, "lead on."

"Which do you prefer?" said the hook-nosed gentleman; "will you go to Whitecross Street, or take up your abode with me, at my residence in Cursitor Street?"

"I say again, lead on! I care not whither," Mr. Wilderspin replied, in a tragical manner.

So of course, the gentleman of the hooked nose, took him to his own residence, where Mr. Wilderspin found himself, for the first time, in durance vile. Here Mr. Wilderspin did as all do who enter the gates of Mr. Nabem; that is to say, he wrote to all his friends, imploring them to come to his assistance. But long and anxiously he paced backwards and forwards, behind the iron bars which enclosed Mr. Nabem's yard, without being gladdened by the sight of a face or the sound of a voice that he knew. It was the old, old story. Poverty had parted good company. When your riches have taken unto themselves wings and flown away, you generally find that your friends have joined the covey. Well, it must be confessed, it is a painful thing to visit a once prosperous friend in adversity. It is not always selfishness or indifference that withholds you. You cannot bear the sight; you have nothing to offer your poor friend; you cannot help him in any way; you are, perhaps, not in a position to take him even a trifling present. So you stop away. Mr. Wilderspin, though recognising these considerations, was nevertheless deeply wounded by the neglect of his friends. As he leant against the bars, waiting in vain for the sight of a familiar face, his heart swelled within him, and the hot tears gushed forth and fell in large drops on the prison flags.

A day's experience of Mr. Nabem's charges for board and lodging brought him to think of a Habeas Corpus. Sixpence per sheet for letter-paper, and everything else in proportion, was clearly an excessive charge, only to be submitted to on the moral conviction that he would get out to-morrow. But, as the prospect of getting out seemed exceedingly dim and distant, Mr. Wilderspin, acting upon the advice of a fellow-prisoner, paid a sum of four pounds for a Habeas Corpus, and was transferred to Her Majesty's Prison of the Bench. Mr. Wilderspin had studied the British Constitution, and knew what a Habeas Corpus was in theory. In actuality he found a Habeas Corpus to be a fat man, of the Jewish persuasion

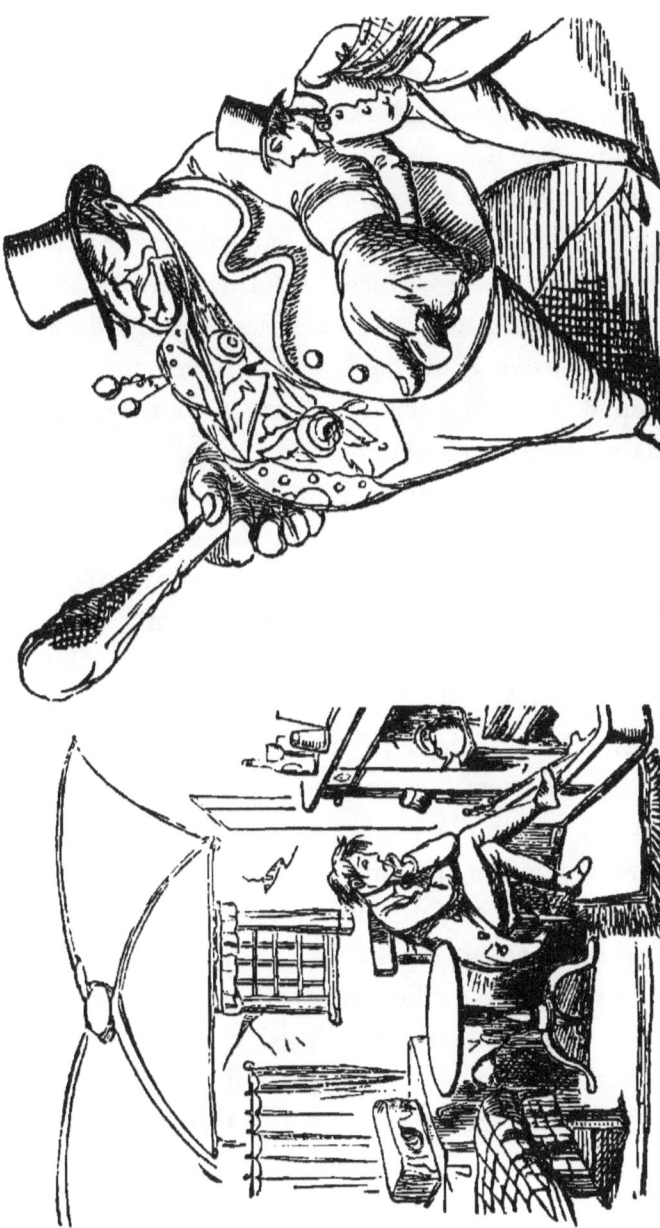

MR. WILDERSPIN TAKES UP HIS RESIDENCE WITH HER
MAJESTY IN HER PALACE OF "THE BENCH."

MR. WILDERSPIN AT LENGTH UNDERSTANDS WHAT IS A "HABEAS CORPUS."

who walked with him had kept his eye upon him during his passage from Cursitor street to Belvidere-place. As to the nature, disposition, and tastes of a Habeas Corpus, he found that he had no objection to old ale, and preferred riding in a cab to walking on foot. Mr. Wilderspin, having been formally handed over by the Habeas Corpus to the Governor of the Queen's Bench Prison, was conducted through a series of guarded doors, into an extensive court-yard, looking not unlike the playground of a large school. Here some fifty or sixty persons were lounging about, smoking, talking, playing at rackets, and appearing to enjoy themselves very much indeed. Mr. Wilderspin saw that the old scholars of this seminary were regarding him as a newly-arrived boy, and, feeling as nervous as the new boy usually does, he was glad to slink away to the cell that had been allotted to him. When Mr. Wilderspin entered his apartment, a cold shudder ran through his frame. It was a cell in reality. The roof was vaulted and whitewashed ; the floor was of a cold black slate, and there was but one small grated window to admit the light. The place was completely destitute of furniture,—there was not even a stone bench to sit upon. Mr. Wilderspin half expected to see a ring in the floor, with a chain attached to it. He was considerably relieved when he found that he was not condemned to occupy this dungeon as it then was. An elderly female, of thin and shrivelled aspect, who offered "to do" for him, informed him that he could have any furniture he pleased, by paying for it.

The ordinary suit of bench furniture consisted of a truckle-bed, a chair, a table, and a square of Kidder-minster carpet, the charge for which, per week, being ten shillings. When the cell was provided with the articles mentioned, and a fire was lighted in the grate, it was by no means so gloomy a place as it at first appeared. Indeed, when night fell, and the view of the bars was shut out by the little curtain which drew across the window, there was scarcely anything to remind Mr. Wilderspin that he was in prison. After his first sad moments, Mr. Wilderspin began to be interested with what he saw around him. The shrivelled female came out and in to attend upon him, just as his own servant did at home. Now it was, "When would you like your tea, sir?" or, "Shall I get you some water-cresses?" Another time, "Shall I fetch your beer, sir?" or, "The post-office is just past the church, sir." The woman spoke to him as if he were free to do what he liked, to have his tea when he liked, his beer when he liked, or to take a walk past the church, to post his letters, when it suited him. And he soon found that the Benchers were free to do all these things, and many others besides, indeed, he could not discover that there was anything the Benchers might not do, except walk more than a hundred and fifty yards in a straight line.

Mr. Wilderspin was pleased to find that there was a great deal of mutual sympathy and fellow-feeling among the Benchers. Two or three heads were popped in at his door, on his first arrival, to inquire if he found himself comfortable, and if he was in need of anything.

His immediate neighbours exhibited a generous rivalry in letting him into the secrets of prison life ; and Mr. Wilderspin found that there were many things in that branch of knowledge which it was essential to his comfort and convenience to be acquainted with, and which it must have taken him a long time to find out for himself.   It was very pleasing to Mr. Wilderspin to find that his fellow-prisoners took so deep an interest in smoothing the path of his pilgrimage in that vale of tears.   A fellow-feeling made them all wondrous kind.

On his appearance on the Grand Parade, next day, every one he met, had a bow and a smile for him ; and, before the day was out, he had shaken hands and fraternised with nearly every man in the prison.

RECEPTION OF MR. WILDERSPIN ON THE GRAND PARADE.

ADVENTURE THE TWENTIETH.

Mr. Wilderspin listens to the fond hopes of the man who has been "going out to-morrow" every day for the last ten years.—The man who doesn't want to go out.—The man of many tailors.— The man who is in for £50,000, but who really does not owe a penny in the world,—"not a penny, sir."—The man who came to grief in consequence of having lit his pipe with a hundred pound note—Party's name, Walker.—The man who has been in for twenty years for contempt of Court, in not answering a polite communication from the Lord Chancellor.—The bold smuggler of the "county side," a party never out of *spirits.*— Mr. Wilderspin, having received his discharge, through the good offices of his friend, Murphy, gives a farewell entertainment to the "Benchers."—Song by the chair: "Wildy, we shall miss you."

THE Queen's Bench Prison presents a phase of life entirely *sui generis.* You cannot see the same sort of thing in other prisons. In fact, it may be said that the Queen's Bench is the Belgravia of Prisondom. It is a privileged place. The denizens pleasantly call it Hudson's Hotel—Hudson being the name of the Governor—and, on writing to their friends, date from Belvidere Place. In country prisons debtors are obliged to wash at a common pump, to clean their own rooms, to make their own beds, and to submit to discipline scarcely less severe than criminals are subjected to

In the London prison of Whitecross Street, they put your pipe out, forbid you candles, and send you to bed, like children, at ten o'clock. No such restrictions prevail in the Queen's Bench. The English debtor's cell there is his castle, and he may do as he likes, so long as he keeps the peace. He may live as luxuriously as his means will allow. He may have any number of friends to visit him. He may go out visiting to neighbouring cells. He may keep high festival, and he may, if his bent be that way, which it often is, indulge in dissipation to his heart's content. True,

THE BOLD SMUGGLER OF THE "COUNTY SIDE," A PARTY NEVER OUT OF SPIRITS.

there are rules and restrictions in the Queen's Bench
Prison, but they interfere with no one. It is laid down
that no prisoner shall be supplied at the prison Tap
with more than one quart of beer a day, yet there is
o difficulty in obtaining half-a-dozen quarts, if you
desire it. Spirits are forbidden in the prison, yet grog
is always to be had. How the spirits come in no one
knows, but there is a tradition that a smuggler on the
county side brings them in over the back wall by means
of an india-rubber tube. As to beer, a poor county
debtor will always be happy to oblige you with his

MR. WILDERSPIN LISTENS TO THE FOND HOPES OF THE MAN WHO HAS BEEN
"GOING OUT TO MORROW" EVERY DAY FOR THE LAST TEN YEARS,

allowance for a consideration. In most cases, a prison, like death, may be said to be a leveller of all distinctions. The fraudulent banker and the burglar both have their hair cropped, and are put into the same livery of grey. But it is not so in the Queen's Bench. Here there is an upper and a lower class—the debtors who can pay for their furnished apartments and are privileged to use the Grand Parade at all times of the day, and the debtors who obtain an allowance from the county, and are not privileged to walk on the Grand Parade except at certain hours. These latter live at the back of the

THE MAN WHO DOESN'T WANT TO GO OUT.

premises, in the slums of prisondom, and are not con
sidered fit company for the aristocrats in front. Indeed, it is an offence against the laws of the prison for
any one living in the front to go behind and visit a
denizen of the back.

For some days Mr. Wilderspin was so diverted, by
the curious state of society in which he found himself,
that he entirely lost sight of his own misfortunes. He
had made many acquaintances, and heard all their his-
tories ; and he noticed that in every single instance the
debtors all declared, in the most solemn manner, that
they did not really owe a penny in the world. They were
all victims of ruthless oppression. Some were in constant
expectation of going out to-morrow ; but they had been
going out to-morrow for years past, and their to-morrow
never came. These were the melancholy people who
took their imprisonment as an injury, and fretted under
it. There were some, however, who were quite content
with their prison life, and did not want to go out.
There were people of a jolly disposition, who had
abundant means, and could afford to live well. The
prison life suited their tastes and habits. The most
notable of this class was a stout middle-aged gentleman,
who had been a railway speculator. He had failed for
an amount which he could never possibly pay ; and, as
his creditors would not allow him to go through the
Court, he dismissed all thoughts of them and his liabilities, and quietly accepted durance as the fixed and
final condition of his existence. He was quite as happy

in the Bench as he had ever been out of it. The chief
object of his life was to feed well, and in the Bench he
could obtain every delicacy of the season. When the
fishmonger, the poulterer, and the butcher, came in,
this gentleman would always be seen inspecting their
stock with the eye of an experienced commissary. He
loved such choice delicacies as a bit of turbot, a phea-
sant, a woodcock, or a brace of partridges, and something of the kind was always to be seen hanging outside the window of his cell. The outskirts of the window is the Bencher's only larder. By looking up,
each one can tell what the other is going to have for
dinner. In August, there will be seen fluttering from
the windows of the Queen's Bench Prison as many
brace of grouse as would stock a gameseller's shop.
In September, the grouse are replaced by partridges ;
later on, the partridges by hares and pheasants.

Society in the Bench is strongly flavoured by elabo-
rately dressed young men, of loud manners and loose
habits ; young men who wear large moustaches, smoke
a great deal from silver-mounted meerschaums, and
devote much of their energies to the obtaining more
than their regular allowance of drink. They are of all
ranks. Occasionally, there is a lord among them,
almost always a baronet ; but most of them are simply
the sons of well-to-do tradesmen ; but whether lords or
commoners, their style of dress, their manners, their
tastes, and their habits are exactly alike. They have
all run through their property, and all much in the

same way, viz. by gambling, racing, yachting, betting, and generally leading a fast life. Their debts are generally enormous, and their schedules, when they are drawn out, might serve as a complete Directory to all the tailors, bootmakers, hosiers, jewellers, wine merchants, cigar sellers, and livery stable-keepers in London. One of these gentlemen was known by the appellation of "the man of many tailors," from the fact that no less than nineteen gentlemen of that trade appeared to oppose him on his first hearing.

Mr. Wilderspin met several gentlemen in the prison whom he had known in the days of their prosperity.

THE MAN OF MANY TAILORS

How the prison life had changed them! Here, for instance, was one who had been a bank director. In a few short weeks he had been transformed from the suave, refined, and gentlemanly man of business, into a slouchy, pipe-smoking, beer-drinking listless idler. The process of demoralization that goes on in the Queen's Bench Prison, is very rapid. Very few men can resist the transmutation. The finest gold becomes tarnished here : the inferior sort turns to base metal. The first symptom of demoralization that shows itself is the habit of constantly wearing slippers. When men

THE MAN WHO IS IN FOR £50,000 BUT WHO REALLY DOES NOT OWE A PENNY IN THE WORLD,—" NOT A PENNY, SIR."

abandon high-heeled boots and take to slippers, they surrender the outwork of their self-respect. That is a maxim that is well understood in the Bench. The newly caged debtor may defend his citadel for a day or two, but at the end of a week he is sure to succumb to slippers. Then he abandons his tall hat, and takes to a wide-awake; he leaves off wearing collars, takes to smoking clay pipes, allows a moustache to grow, and troubleth himself about beer. Mr. Wilderspin found himself yielding to the baneful influence of a prison, like all the others. He took to slippers, wide-awakes, clay pipes, beer — everything but a moustache, the growth of which not even debt and imprisonment were potent enough to promote.

Mr. Wilderspin had heard much of the hardship of imprisonment for debt; but from all he heard and saw in the Queen's Bench, he was decidedly of opinion that there were very few persons there who did not richly deserve the durance which they suffered. There were exceptions, but they were very few. There was a man who had come to grief in consequence of his having accidentally lit his pipe with a hundred-pound note, which he was about to devote to the payment of his creditors; but his appearance did not warrant entire credence of his story. The case of a poor, old, broken-down man, who had been in prison for twenty years, was really a hard one. It was a case of Contempt of Court. The poor old fellow told the story to every new comer. The Lord Chancellor had ordered him to restore a horse, which had died of the glanders a year previously. "My Lord," he said, "I cannot restore the horse." "But you must," said the Lord Chancellor. "My Lord, the horse has been dead these twelve months." "I cannot help that; you must restore him." "It is impossible, my Lord; it can't be done." "Very well; I commit you for Contempt of Court." And so the poor man was sent to prison until he could restore the horse, which was dead, and had probably been dispersed in halfpenny-worths of dog's-meat, or been consumed long ago in sausages. He might have got out if he would have signed some paper which was presented to him; but he had got into so much trouble through signing papers, that nothing would induce him to sign his name to anything.

Mr. Wilderspin, like most people who get into the Queen's Bench, made no immediate effort to get out again. Prisoners generally have a vague belief that they will be restored to liberty, in some way or other, before the first week is out. How it is to be done they have no definite idea; but the prevalent feeling is, that some friend will come to their assistance, or that their creditors will be induced to come to terms. But if the truth must be told, friends very rarely fulfil the expectations that are entertained of them in such cases, and there is probably no instance of a creditor coming to terms after securing the person of his debtor. When Mr. Wilderspin saw no prospect of relief from these sources he resolved to "go through the Court." His

fellow-prisoners all applauded his resolve, and gave him
much valuable advice for his guidance in the process of
going through.   The man of many tailors, who had
great experience in the matter, implored him, whatever
he did, not to go before Mr. Crabtree, who would be
sure to send him back.   "Manage to go up before old
Earthapple, my dear boy, and you will be all safe.
Earthapple is the commissioner for my money. Phi-
lander is not so bad, only he is apt to have quarrels with
his wife, and then he spits his spite on the insolvent,
and gives him a month, perhaps." So, in due time,

THE MAN WHO CAME TO GRIEF IN CONSEQUENCE OF HIS HAVING LIT HIS
PIPE WITH A HUNDRED POUND NOTE.—PARTY'S NAME, WALKER.

Mr. Wilderspin filed his schedule, and went up, as good luck would have it, before the pet Commissioner, Mr. Earthapple. It was said that Mr. Commissioner Earthapple sat with his own protection in his pocket, and that he could not have sat in safety without it. That fact, perhaps, accounted for the fellow feeling which he displayed for the insolvents who came up before him. Mr. Wilderspin was opposed by several creditors. When one stood forward, Mr. Commissioner Earthapple asked him what he had to say.

THE MAN WHO HAS BEEN IN FOR TWENTY YEARS FOR CONTEMPT OF COURT, IN NOT ANSWERING A POLITE COMMUNICATION FROM THE LORD CHANCELLOR.

Well ; the creditor wanted his money.

"No doubt you do," said Mr. Commissioner Earth-apple ; but this is not a Court for paying Creditors, but for relieving debtors of their liabilities."

Mr. Commissioner Earthapple would not allow any opposition to bar Mr. Wilderspin's passage through his Court ; and he would not even allow Mr. Wilderspin to say he was ashamed of the humiliating position in which he stood.

"Humiliating position, sir," he roared out indignantly ; "are you aware, sir, that some of the most distinguished men of the day, have been glad to accept the protection of this Court ? Take a first class certificate, your schedule is highly creditable to you."

It is by no means a rare occurrence for prisoners, when they have been liberated, to return to the Bench to take farewell of their fellow-prisoners : and it is to the credit of the Benchers that they always rejoice most heartily when one of their number is set free. Mr. Wilderspin returned the same evening, and met a select number of the Benchers in the room of the man of many tailors, where high festival was kept up until the bell rang for visitors to depart, when Mr. Wilderspin shook hands with all his old friends and fellow-prisoners, and quitted the Queen's Bench.

The same persons would not rejoice at the prosperity of each other out of prison. As neighbours, they would probably be jealous of each other. As a rule, Smith, the grocer, being himself in difficulties, would

not be apt to rush off and congratulate Brown the ironmonger, on being freed from *his* embarrassments. In
the friendly feeling among prisoners, we have a tacit
admission, that the loss of liberty is one of the direst
calamities.

MR. WILDERSPIN HAVING RECEIVED HIS DISCHARGE, THROUGH THE GOOD OFFICES OF HIS FRIEND, MURPHY, GIVES A FAREWELL ENTERTAIN-
MENT TO THE "BENCHERS."   SONG BY THE CHAIR—" WILDY WE SHALL MISS YOU."

ADVENTURE THE TWENTY-FIRST.

Mr. Wilderspin, being desirous to make himself acquainted with the holiday manners and customs of the people, embarks for Greenwich, and makes the acquaintance of a young female of prepossessing appearance.—Mr. Wilderspin, finding himself at Greenwich, does as the Greenwichers do.—Mr. Wilderspin, in company with the "female of prepossessing appearance," makes the descent of Mont Greenwich.—Mr. Wilderspin listens to an authentic account of the death of Nelson, related by an eye-witness, who will be "happy to drink Mr. Wilderspin's health."—Tea and shrimps, Ninepence.—Mr. Wilderspin, as he appeared on the evening of the eventful day, owing to the "regular young man" of the female of prepossessing appearance.

A CERTAIN Captain, a roaring blade, who made songs and sang them in the good old days of George the Third, has chronicled in verse an infinite variety of excuses for drinking. The moral of that song is, that whatever you love to do, you can always find an excuse for doing. Thus Mr. Wilderspin, in coming out of prison, had little difficulty in persuading himself that what he wanted was a little fresh air and recreation. The restraint of a parliamentary life had cramped the natural man ; and his period of durance, though short, had left a sense of oppression on his spirits, which he was desirous to shake

T

off. Had he argued the matter with himself, he would possibly have been convinced that his first duty was to inquire into his affairs and set his house in order; but knowing that that would be the conclusion to which he would come, if he did argue with himself, he resolved not to risk the mental discussion. Most people, in desperate circumstances, give themselves up to impulse. The gambler risks his last guinea with almost complete indifference as to what may be the turn of the die. The toper spends his last shilling when he does not know where to get a penny. The failing speculator generally enters upon a grander enterprise than any he has yet ventured when he finds he is upon the point of bankruptcy. Mr. Wilderspin was in the position of all three. He lacked the courage to face his position. The philosophy on which he prided himself oozed out at his fingers' ends, just when he wanted it. Was there ever a practical philosopher in this world? Never! Your philosopher, who can lecture you upon the impolicy of getting into debt, and the means of avoiding it, is himself "over head and ears" in liability. Have you not known the philosopher who reads you a solemn lecture upon the baneful practice of drinking, get "mortal" over the lecture, and eventually illustrate his precepts by an exhibition of himself in a state of utter helplessness? Philosophers are like the fools who build houses. The benefit of their labours is reaped by others. The real practical philosopher is the man who has acquired wisdom without knowing that wisdom is a science. If we would only abolish that word philosophy, and substitute the word common-sense, perhaps we should have more practical wisdom in the world.

The excuse which Mr. Wilderspin made for himself, when he resolved to take a day's holiday at Greenwich, was, that he would be enabled to study the holiday manners and customs of the lower orders of the people. Such knowledge might be useful to him, for he did not despair of regaining his position as a Member of Parliament. His experience had taught him that it was no easy thing to crush a man out of the parliamentary arena once he had been within it. An M.P. may lose his election, or he may be unseated on petition; but having been once an M.P., he is still in the market, and the next general election is sure to restore him to Parliament. It is the same with Ministers of State—once a Cabinet Minister, always a Cabinet Minister, when the turn of your party comes. The most common-place men make great reputations in consequence of these opportunities. Lord Jones having had a seat in every Cabinet since the beginning of the century, and a finger in all the great measures which his party had been forced to carry during that time, is a great Statesman, as a matter of course. Lord Jones is one of our great men; his name is a household word—we quote him as an authority; but as he is destined to be a Cabinet Minister to the end of the chapter, we shall never find out what a mediocre man he is, unless he expose himself to the enemy by writing a book, or doing something else which will put him into comparison with ordinary men on fair terms.

So Mr. Wilderspin went forth to study the manners and habits of the people, with the view of making himself acquainted with their claims to the franchise, in case he should some day have to take part in the discussion of Parliamentary Reform. Meeting a young lady of prepossessing appearance on board the Green-

MR. WILDERSPIN BEING DESIROUS TO MAKE HIMSELF ACQUAINTED WITH THE HOLIDAY MANNERS AND CUSTOMS OF THE PEOPLE, EMBARKS FOR GREENWICH, AND MAKES THE ACQUAINTANCE OF A YOUNG FEMALE OF PREPOSSESSING APPEARANCE.

wich boat, his political mission was soon driven out of his head. Having satisfied himself that the young lady was unaccompanied by any male friend, Mr. Wilderspin made bold to pay her marked and special attention. To this she did not object, but received his compliments and his bottled stout with evident pleasure. Mr. Wilderspin found in this young lady a pleasing study. To what rank of life she belonged it would have been hard

MR. WILDERSPIN FINDING HIMSELF AT GREENWICH, DOES AS THE GREENWICHERS DO.

to say from a mere casual glance. Her skin was deli
cate, her clothes were elegant, her manner ladylike, and
her hand small and neatly gloved. She might have
been a countess, could it have been possible to imagine
a countess going for a day's holiday by herself in the
Greenwich boat. Mr. Wilderspin's philosophical mind
found food for much entertaining reflection in the contrast which this lady presented to others of her sex on
the boat. It was a pet theory of his that it was a shame
to marry pretty girls. He had known so many pretty
girls who had been married, and utterly spoilt by the
process. He had seen the bright face in a few short
months become shadowed by sadness; the neat dressing,
the nicely-fitting gown, and the natty boots degenerate
into sloppy wrappers and down-at-heel slippers. And
then the baby!!!

"There are plenty ugly and plain women to marry,"
Mr. Wilderspin was wont to say; "why don't the fellows
marry them and let those pretty girls alone to bloom
for ever." Mr. Wilderspin had another theory, and I
venture to think not an absurd one. It was, that while
pretty girls were spoilt by matrimony, plain and ugly
ones are improved by it. Upon these premises, he
argued, logically enough, that it was better to marry the
plain woman than the pretty one, since the former by
the improvement of her charms, promoted an increase
of love, while the latter by her deterioration, caused an
exhaustion of that feeling. The young lady whom Mr.
Wilderspin met on board the Greenwich boat was one

of the pretty ones, whom he would have thought it
sacrilege to marry. Did he not go upon Blackheath
and engage in a donkey race with her? I should like
to know, if he had married her next day, if they would
ever have gone donkey racing again. Did she not race
down Greenwich Hill with him, and laugh good
humouredly when they both stumbled and rolled over
each other to the bottom? Would she have laughed if
he had so disarranged her crinoline a month or two after
marriage? And would Mr. Wilderspin himself have
cared to join in such sport then? It is wonderful how
much interest you can take in a woman when you are
courting her. You are never tired of going about with
her; of taking her to see this, that, and the other; of
listening to her simple chatter. When after years of
married life, during which that lovely creature has
become fat, and got into the habit of having a baby once
a year, you look back to your courting days, you wonder
how you could have done all the silly and tiresome
things which you did. Silly and tiresome they seem to
you now. Delightful things they were in the days of
your embroidered shirt and straw-coloured gloves.

Greenwich Park is an excellent place for love making.
On ordinary days, there are a hundred shady banks
where you can sit, like Virgil's shepherd, under the
shadow of the spreading beeches, secure from the observation of all but the pensioners. It is the business
of the pensioners not to let lovers alone. They spy
them out with their telescopes, follow them up, and

MR. WILDERSPIN, IN COMPANY WITH THE "FEMALE OF PREPOSSESSING APPEARANCE," MAKES THE DESCENT OF MONT GREENWICH

MR. WILDERSPIN LISTENS TO AN AUTHENTIC ACCOUNT OF THE DEATH OF NEL-
SON, RELATED BY AN EYE-WITNESS, WHO WILL BE HAPPY TO DRINK MR.
WILDERSPIN'S HEALTH.

contrive to stumble upon them as if by accident.   The
" price of a pint of beer " will deliver you of their
company ; but if you do not disburse that amount of
your own accord, and at once, you will be condemned
to hear a long and circumstantial account of the death of
Nelson, at which melancholy occurrence it would appear
that every pensioner in Greenwich Hospital was present.
Mr. Wilderspin, being naturally of an enquiring turn,
stood the fire of their stories with great good humour,
and was pleased to find that his charming companion

was interested in the great naval hero. It appeared, however, that the separate identity of Nelson and Wellington were not very well defined in her mind. Ignorance of this kind in a pretty women is always charming. With what delight you set yourself to teach her and put her right. When Mr. Wilderspin retired with his fair companion to a "nice back parlour" to partake of the staple refreshment of Greenwich—viz., tea and shrimps

—he fully explained to her which was Nelson and which was Wellington. In return for this information, the young lady instructed Mr. Wilderspin how to peel shrimps, and take perriwinkles out of their shells with a pin. The last-mentioned accomplishment was really worth knowing. Mr. Wilderspin had never been able to get perriwinkles out of their holes without breaking their tails ; but his lady friend showed him a scientific manner of screwing them out whole and intact. Thus it might be said, that the fair one gave Mr. Wilderspin his *quid pro quo* in point of useful information ; and it was certainly of more importance for him to know how to take perriwinkles out of their shells than for her to know which was Nelson and which was Wellington.

Mr. Wilderspin spent a delightful day with his charming companion ; but his happiness was destined, at a late hour of the evening, to come to wreck. Just as he was offering his arm to the lady to conduct her to the boat, a young man, in a sky-blue waistcoat with gold sprigs, stepped up to him, and demanded, in a menacing tone, what he was doing with that 'ere young woman ? And before Mr. Wilderspin could reply, the young man in the sky-blue waistcoat hit him a succession of blows on the face, which left him almost destitute of the power of vision. Meantime the young lady had screamed and fainted in the arms of the young man, who it appeared, was her accepted lover. Finding himself in this delicate situation, Mr. Wilderspin made the best of his way home by himself, bearing with him a souvenir of his

day in Greenwich Park with the lovely unknown, in the
shape of a black eye.

MR. WILDERSPIN, AS HE APPEARED ON THE EVENING OF THE EVENTFUL DAY,
OWING TO THE "REGULAR YOUNG MAN" OF THE FEMALE OF PREPOSSESSING
APPEARANCE.

ADVENTURE THE TWENTY-SECOND.

Mr. Wilderspin, having exhausted at once, the pleasures of life and his fortune, is troubled with gloomy thoughts.—Takes refuge from his troubles in the arms of Morpheus, and recalls the happy scenes of his childhood.—Ah! the waking hour, Mr. Wilderspin is presented with a long bill by his landlady!—Mr. Wilderspin exposes his unhappy financial position, but fails to mollify the stony heart of the stern Widow Jenkins.—Goes upon another tack and succeeds better.—Mr. Wilderspin having popped everything (including the weasel), at length pops "the question."—Mr. Wilderspin settles accounts with the worthy Mrs. Jenkins by leading her to the Altar of Hymen.

SWEET are the uses of adversity. The waggoner on the high road of life bestows no thought upon Hercules, until his cart is upset in the ditch; then he sitteth down weeping, and crieth aloud for the god to help him. It is only when our carts are upset that we begin to see our folly, and feel what miserable sinners we are. Some require a repetition of misfortune to bring them to their senses; but there are very few indeed whom persistent calamity cannot bring to their marrow-bones. There is no more edifying repentance than that of the man who is condemned to be hanged. He, the most guilty of men, might be envied by the most pious; for he knoweth that he shall surely die next Monday at eight o'clock, when, having duly prayed and repented in the meantime, he will go straight to glory. So the Chaplain assures him ; and so he believes. As for the good man, who keepeth the commandments, he owns that he is a sinner every minute of his life, and may fall down dead, or be run over, before he has time to settle his last accounts. Under these circumstances, it might be logically contended that the surest road to heaven, is up the steps of the scaffold.

Mr. Wilderspin, like the occupant of the condemned cell, did not come to repentance until all was lost. A cheque which he had drawn upon his bankers was returned one morning, marked, "No effects." His fortune was exhausted. Like a prodigal son, he had wasted the substance bequeathed to him by his respected uncle, in riotous living—or if not exactly in riotous living, at least by thoughtless and reckless expenditure. No man was more ready than Mr. Wilderspin to lecture his fellows upon the virtue of prudence ; yet in his own practice he had been the most imprudent of men. A sum of money which he might have profitably invested in the Funds, or in business, he had recklessly dissipated, living upon the capital instead of the interest. True, he had sunk a small sum in a Welsh coal company ; but that money, like the coal, was sunk so deep, that there was no prospect of its ever being dug up again.

When Mr. Wilderspin contemplated the utter ruin in which he had involved himself, he was struck with deep remorse, and like a true philosopher, gave way to thoughts of self-destruction. There was no consoling circumstance in his position. If he looked back, he saw a desert strewn with wasted opportunities—the skeletons of his good resolutions. If he looked forward, the prospect was a vast darkness unrelieved by one ray of hope. His Present was a mere standing-point between that reproachful past and a cheerless future.

Mr. Wilderspin resolved upon self-destruction, and at once provided himself with a revolver and a bottle of sherry. He sat until midnight, wrapped in gloomy thoughts. The night was in unison with the dark deed which he contemplated. The rain dashed in fitful splashes against his window; the wind howled and shrieked among the chimney-tops; and in the intervals of dead silence which occurred when the tempest had spent its fury, Mr. Wilderspin could hear in the ticking of the clock, the steady and onward tramp of the last minutes which were left him upon earth. Ten—eleven —a quarter past! half-past! three quarters past!— TWELVE !!! At the first stroke of the bell, Mr Wilderspin laid his hand upon the pistol; at the sixth stroke, he cocked it; at the ninth, he levelled the weapon at his head; as the last sounded, he pulled the trigger. No report followed; Mr. Wilderspin felt not the deadly ball—the pistol had missed fire! On examining it, he found that he had forgotten to put on a cap; on further inquiry, he found that he had forgotten to load the weapon; and further still, that he had omitted to provide himself with powder and ball. He would have gone out and procured some, but it was past midnight, and the shops were shut. What was to be done? As Mr. Wilderspin cast his glance around in search of some other instrument of destruction, his eye fell upon the bottle of sherry. Luckily it happened to be South African. Without a moment's hesitation he opened the bottle, poured out a tumbler of its contents, and drained it off. With terrible desperation he filled and drained another tumbler almost the

MR. WILDERSPIN, HAVING EXHAUSTED AT ONCE THE PLEASURES OF LIFE AND HIS FORTUNE IS TROUBLED WITH GLOOMY THOUGHTS.

TAKES REFUGE FROM HIS TROUBLES IN THE ARMS OF MORPHEUS, AND RECALLS THE HAPPY SCENES OF HIS CHILDHOOD.

next moment. For an instant he sat with fixed eyes, staring at vacancy. Presently the muscles of the lower part of his face became contracted, as if with nausea ; his frame began to collapse, and his features to assume a deadly pallor. At last, with a terrible groan he fell from his chair, and rolled under the table—not quite dead, but very nearly. Waking up about four in the morning, Mr. Wilderspin was not a little relieved to find, that though under the table, he was still in the land of the living. So he rolled into bed, and, in the soft arms of Morpheus, recalled the happy scenes of his childhood, where he was once more a boy in corduroys, engaging in innocent games with the companions of his youth.

What an uncomfortable thing it is to wake up from a pleasant dream to the unpleasant realities of life !—say, from a *tête-à-tête* with Julia in a honeysuckle bower, to the presence of an officer of the Sheriff, who salutes you with a request to dress and go with him. Ah ! that waking hour !

When Mr. Wilderspin went down to breakfast next morning, he found his landlady waiting to present him with a long bill, for board and lodging, and money lent. The humiliating truth must be told ; Mr. Wilderspin's necessities had driven him to borrow small sums from time to time from his landlady, on the familiar plea of not having change, or having forgotten to draw a cheque. When one has money transactions of this kind with his landlady or his servant, he must necessarily sink some of his dignity, and admit those persons to a greater degree of familiarity than is usual between master and servant. Most persons who have paid rent—or rather, who have not paid rent—will have observed, that protracted non-payment of rent greatly diminishes the distant courtesy which their landlady has preserved towards them at more punctual periods. The gentle tap at the door becomes a rude and hasty knocking. The knives and forks are banged upon the table. The fire-irons are savagely clattered when the

AH! THE WAKING HOUR—MR. WILDERSPIN IS PRESENTED WITH A LONG BILL BY HIS LANDLADY ! MR WILDERSPIN EXPOSES HIS UNHAPPY FINANCIAL POSITION, BUT, FAILS TO MOLLIFY THE STONY HEART OF THE STERN WIDOW JENKINS.

fire-place is swept up ; and a studied delay is observed
in answering the street door.   Mr. Wilderspin had been
subject to these indications of dissatisfaction for some
length of time, and now, at length, the respected Widow
Jenkins had come to the point with him.   She had
her rent to pay—(another form of the heavy bill which
the tradesman has so frequently to make up)—and she
could wait no longer.   Mr. Wilderspin had no resource
left but to reveal his unhappy financial position, and
appeal to the feelings of the widow.

Now, Mrs. Jenkins was not a bad-hearted woman,
but she liked to have her money, and she was not, at

GOES UPON ANOTHER TACK, AND SUCCEEDS BETTER.

first, disposed to allow her feelings to be worked upon. The consequence was, that Mr. Wilderspin had to withstand a great deal of bitter reproach, the burden of which was, that a considerable portion of the bill was for money lent,—actually out of pocket,—and that that circumstance made the case all the more hard, inasmuch as she, Mrs. Jenkins, was an unprotected woman, with no one to speak up for her and protect her rights.

Overwhelmed by these reproaches, Mr. Wilderspin sat down and tore his hair; and then, when he had quite done, Widow Jenkins, giving way to a sense of her unprotected position, sat down in another chair

MR. WILDERSPIN, HAVING POPPED EVERYTHING (INCLUDING THE WEASEL) AT
LENGTH POPS "THE QUESTION."

and sobbed, dropping large tears over Mr. Wilderspin's bill.

Mr. W., unable to contemplate the spectacle of her
grief, at length drew his chair towards the weeping
widow, and whispered, in pathetic accents,—"You
surely would not turn me out in the street, Mrs. Jenkins!" He took her hand as he said these words.

The widow looked at him through her tears, and in a
kindly tone replied, "No; she did not want to do
that."

A brilliant thought struck Mr. Wilderspin at that
moment. Mrs. Jenkins was a widow; though stout,
not bad-looking; possessed a freehold house, and had
money in the Funds; while he, Mr. Wilderspin, was
single, penniless, and her debtor. These circumstances
presented themselves to Mr. Wilderspin's mind in the
shape of a proposition to be worked out to a satisfactory
result. He saw the problem at a glance, and intuitively
felt that he was master of its details. It was just as if
some one had "given" him a straight line on the black
board, and told him to describe an equilateral triangle
upon it. Without going further into the problem which
was proposed by this contrast, Mr. Wilderspin seized
the widow's hand and fell at her feet. What Mr. Wilderspin would have done had he been interrupted at
that moment, and allowed time to reflect upon the step
he was about to take, will never be known; for the
widow there and then accepted him as her affianced
husband.

The problem was solved. *Quod erat demonstran-dum.*

By a very strange coincidence, on the very day that Mr. Wilderspin led the widow Jenkins to the Hymeneal altar, coal was found in the Welsh mine, and the shares went up to a premium.

MR. WILDERSPIN SETTLES ACCOUNTS WITH THE WORTHY MRS. JENKINS BY LEADING HER TO THE
ALTAR OF HYMEN.

ADVENTURE THE TWENTY-THIRD AND LAST.

A picture of domestic bliss—the day after marriage.—Look upon
this picture.—And upon this!—Six weeks after marriage.—Mr.
Wilderspin returns from his club (the Cherokees) to the wife of
his bosom—Time, 2·30 a. m.—Mr. Wilderspin receives a severe
lecture on his unloving conduct, and is dared to continue a Cherokee.—Mr. Wilderspin's pipe is put out—and, of course Mr.
Wilderspin is put out himself.—Mr. Wilderspin, being at length
totally subdued, yields up his latch key and his liberty.—And
lives happily ever afterwards, to see grow up around him an
amiable family, distinguished, no less by the talents of their
father, than by the graces of their accomplished mother.

UNTIL a very late period, it was usual for the novelist
to drop the curtain upon his hero and heroine when he
had brought them safely through all their troubles, and
placed them side by side at the hymeneal altar. As to
what followed, the curiosity of the reader, if any remained, was supposed to be perfectly satisfied with a
general statement to the effect, that the young couple
lived happily ever afterwards. In these days, however,
it has become the fashion to do the marrying about the
middle of the second volume, and give us a peep of
Edward and Lucy in the married and settled state ; nay,
some authors, desiring that the machinery of their art
may be entirely novel in construction and action, have
gone so far as to begin Chapter I. just when Lucy has

presented Edward with the first baby.   Which of these
courses I should pursue had I my own choice, I am not
prepared to say; but any hesitation that I might have
in the matter is disposed of by the fact, that I have
brought the Adventures of Mr. Wilderspin down to the
present moment of his life.   Whatever, then, I may
have to add in this chapter must be entirely of a prophetic nature.   I may say that I truly believe that Mr.
Wilderspin will live happily henceforward ; at the same
time, I cannot reject the conviction that his cup of
sweetness will be occasionally embittered, as is the case

A PICTURE OF DOMESTIC BLISS—THE DAY AFTER MARRIAGE.

with all who are destined to drain the cup of matrimony
to the dregs. That, for the first week or two, he and
his comely bride will present a picture of domestic
bliss, I feel morally certain.

I suppose it may be safely said, that no pair who ever
were married fell out or quarrelled during the first three
days of their honeymoon. Perhaps this supposition
may convict me of entertaining too good an opinion of
human nature ; but that is an error on the right side,
and I prefer adhering to my conviction. On the other
hand, I don't believe that any pair ever got over six
months of their married life without unpleasantnesses
of a more or less serious kind. I am so convinced of
this that—having Mr. Wilderspin's case in my eye—I
can distinctly see a vision of Mrs. W. sitting up at two
o'clock in the morning, waiting for her husband, prepared to hurl an avalanche of reproaches upon his head.
I have seen a great many young men pass from the
chrysalis state of bachelorhood into the butterfly condition of matrimony (or, is it *vice versâ?*), and I have
observed that, in most cases, devotion to the domestic
hearth lasts little more than six months. The clubs,
which for half a year or so have known them not, once
more resound to the sound of their jovial voices. The
abandoned pipe or cigar is once more taken into favour ;
the social glass is restored to its orbit round the maho-
gany, and the voice of the minstrel, so long dumb or
subdued, is heard in the land once more. This of
course, involves stopping out very late, and going home,

AND UPON THIS {—SIX WEEKS AFTER MARRIAGE.

LOOK UPON THIS PICTURE—

at unseemly hours, smelling of tobacco, and occasionally
partially deprived of the power of speech and locomo-
tion.   I wonder what per-centage of wives take this
sort of thing quietly.   If I might venture to express
an opinion, I should say, not an eighth—no, not one in
a million.   I had better come to that at once.   They
are all indignant, and they all demonstrate in some way
or other.   One is good with her tongue ; another with
her nails ; another is as cutting as any by her silence.
It depends upon the husband's quality of skin what
effect it takes upon him.   That the whole race of hus-

MR. WILDERSPIN RETURNS FROM HIS CLUB (THE CHEROKEES) TO THE WIFE OF
HIS BOSOM —TIME, 2 30 A. M.

bands dread that hour of reproach, and regard it as
the misery of their lives, I conscientiously believe; but
its deterring influence is, I am afraid, slight, for what
we love to do we don't mind suffering for.   But Mr.
Wilderspin having married a stout widow considerably
his senior, I can foresee that he will prove the weaker
vessel, and that when he has come home once or twice
at a very late hour, with a short pipe in his mouth, and
his hair over his eyes, he will be induced to indulge in
reflection with wholesome effect as respects his habits.
The process by which he will be brought to this frame
of mind is, no doubt familiar to all who have married

MR. WILDERSPIN RECEIVES A SEVERE LECTURE ON HIS UN-LOVING CONDUCT.
AND IS DARED TO CONTINUE A CHEROKEE.

stout widows of advanced age and active temperament.

The citadel of a mild man's independence is soon
made to capitulate when his defences are vigorously attacked in rapid succession. When he returns at the
small hours, in the state indicated, to seize him by the
throat in the passage, and knock his head against the
barometer, is a very good way of beginning the as-
sault. Follow this up with a harassing curtain lecture
until cockcrow, and alternate your abuse of him with
spasmodic sobbings and regrets that you ever married
him. Open your great guns upon him at breakfast
time, and keep him under a galling fire until after
dinner, when, if he attempt to smoke, seize all his pipes
and smash them up—and there you have him, my
buxom widow! There is one thing to be said, however, madam; this mild, plastic husband of yours, will
never like you. He will stop at home to keep the peace
and save appearances, but he will be inwardly thankful
when he sees you screwed down in your coffin. He
will mourn you, of course, and try and persuade himself that he was really attached to you: but, ten to one
if he does not revenge himself upon you by marrying
the mildest young lady he can find to have him. I
foresee that Mr. Wilderspin will have to submit to the
ordeal I have described; but, from what I know of
him, I feel confident that he will come out of it a
wiser, if a sadder, man; and that when he has sur-
rendered his latch-key to his better half, the door of

happiness in the bosom of his family will ever stand open to him.   Although I have said very harsh things of stout widows in general, I am happy to be able to make an exception in the case of Mrs. Wilderspin, *neè* Jenkins.   This lady, having achieved the victory in the matrimonial battle, shows moderation in her triumph.   Having vanquished the foe, she has no desire to trample on him.   She has no objection to Mr. Wilderspin enjoying his cigar at his own fireside ; nor is she at all exacting in limiting the number of friends he may choose to invite.   She does not even object to her husband "keeping it up" until two in the morning,

MR. WILDERSPIN'S PIPE IS PUT OUT — AND OF COURSE MR. WILDERSPIN IS
PUT OUT HIMSELF.

if she be there to do her share of the honours and participate in the festivities. I think, therefore, there is no probability of Mr. Wilderspin hating her, and feeling relieved when he sees her quietly inurned. I am sure, if you were to hint such a thing to him, he would feel very much shocked.

It just strikes me that the point at which I have arrived in this prophetic sketch of Mr. Wilderspin's career would be the best period for novelists to drop the curtain upon their heroes and heroines. Having seen the result of the battle which always ensues upon the honeymoon, they would be better able to judge if Ed-

MR. WILDERSPIN BEING AT LENGTH TOTALLY SUBDUED, YIELDS UP HIS LATCH-KEY AND HIS LIBERTY.

ward and Lucy were likely to live happily ever afterwards or not. As to my own hero, I feel fully warranted in assuring the reader that he will live happily

MR. WILDERSPIN LIVES HAPPILY EVER AFTERWARDS, TO SEE GROW UP AROUND HIM AN AMIABLE FAMILY, DISTINGUISHED, NO LESS BY THE TALENTS OF THEIR FATHER, THAN BY THE GRACES OF THEIR ACCOMPLISHED MOTHER.

henceforward to see grow up around him an amiable family, distinguished no less by the talents of their father than by the graces of their accomplished mother, and that when he dies, he will be deeply lamented by a large circle of sorrowing friends.

www.ingramcontent.com/pod-product-compliance
Lightning Source LLC
Chambersburg PA
CBHW020953030726
47496CB00005B/1485